"Divorces aren't given in seconds, you know."

Cathy bit her lip. "I've thought of that. All I ask is that you cooperate. Set me free, Jarrold."

"If that's what you really want."

"Thank you." She tried to sound pleased. "I'll go and tell Stewart, and then we'll be off. *This isn't happening,* she thought. *Once we promised to be together forever. What happened to us?* She looked at her husband awkwardly, and her words came out in a voice suddenly cracked. "I suppose this is goodbye."

"Not quite yet," Jarrod said crisply. "I said you'd get my consent. I didn't say I'd give it today."

"What do you mean?" She stared at him uncomprehendingly, apprehension creeping along her spine.

"Stay," he said. "I'll give you my consent a week from now."

Books by Rosemary Carter

HARLEQUIN PRESENTS

HARLEQUIN ROMANCE

These books may be available at your local bookseller.

Don't miss any of our special offers. Write to us at the following address for information on our newest releases.

Harlequin Reader Service
P.O. Box 52040, Phoenix, AZ 85072-2040
Canadian address: P.O. Box 2800, Postal Station A,
5170 Yonge St., Willowdale, Ont. M2N 6J3

ROSEMARY CARTER

a forever affair

Harlequin Books

TORONTO • NEW YORK • LONDON
AMSTERDAM • PARIS • SYDNEY • HAMBURG
STOCKHOLM • ATHENS • TOKYO • MILAN

Harlequin Presents first edition February 1986
ISBN 0-373-10855-9

Original hardcover edition published in 1985
by Mills & Boon Limited

CHAPTER ONE

'I DON'T know what to say.' Cathy looked up, dazed and a little confused.

'That you'll marry me of course,' Stewart said.

Cathy glanced down at the colour-chart in her hand. Until a few minutes ago her life had been ordered, peaceful. If not happy. The Fairchild house was coming on well. In the remodelled living-room the pale striped wallpaper lent just the right touch to the new gold carpet and the chairs which had been recovered in brushed velvet. Mrs Fairchild was so satisfied with the way things were going that she had said she would tell her friends about her decorator, and would give them the name of the firm where Cathy worked. A decided morale-booster for a girl who was practically still making her debut in the field.

And then five minutes ago Stewart had walked into the dining-room where Cathy was trying to decide on the right paint for the ceiling. As the architect in charge of the extensive remodelling of the house she had thought he had come to inspect the progress of the work.

Instead he had said, 'Cathy, will you marry me?'

'I'm already married,' she protested.

'In name only.'

He reached for her hand as he drew her gently against him. 'I love you, Cathy. I want you to be my wife.'

'I'm married,' she said again.

'It's time you filed for a divorce.'

'This is the oddest proposal,' she said, playing for time. 'Amidst colour-charts and sheet-covered furniture. Why didn't you ask me the other night, when we went out for dinner?'

'Because I didn't want to rush things then.'

'Or tomorrow, on our way to the art exhibition?'

'Because time is suddenly of the essence. It's as I told you, darling. I only heard yesterday about the assignment.'

'You did say Canada?'

'Toronto, yes. And I want you with me when I go.'

Canada. How far was Canada from South Africa? Thousands of miles. Thousands of miles between her and Jarrod.

'Well, Cathy?'

'I can't give you an answer so quickly.' She stared up at him, big green eyes wide with distress.

'Darling, you can't be surprised. You must have known how I felt about you.'

She had known. And though she did not feel the same way about him—would she ever feel that way about any man again?—she had nevertheless allowed him to go on seeing her. Wrong of her perhaps, but she had been lonely and unhappy, and Stewart was a kind and understanding friend.

'I knew you wanted a relationship,' she admitted.

'I tried hard enough to get you into bed.'

She smiled. 'And I said no.' She remembered the two incidents only too well. But they hadn't bothered her, and she had been able to refuse him with tact.

'But now we're talking marriage,' Stewart said.

'Commitment,' Cathy murmured.

After a moment Stewart said, 'The two go together.'

'Yes . . .'

He gave her a strange look. 'Have you never thought about it?'

'If I did, it wasn't consciously. I couldn't, Stewart, you know that.'

'And now?'

His tone was gentle, but there was a hint of tension in the arm around her shoulders.

'Can you give me time?' Cathy asked at last, and the words seemed wrenched from the very centre of her being.

'There's so little time.'

'I understand.'

'I can't delay the trip. It's the chance of a lifetime. If the people out there are happy with my designs there will be more work.'

'It's a chance you can't refuse,' Cathy conceded warmly.

'There's no telling when I'd be returning to Johannesburg, when I'd be able to see you again.' He paused. 'This is a shock to you, I can see that. But you must have known that sooner or later you'd have to make a decision about your life.'

Months ago she had made some decisions. She had completed the decorating course she'd started so long ago, and had found a job. She had taken a new flat. She had learned, painfully, to live on her own once again.

'You haven't seen Jarrod for almost a year,' Stewart said.

'I know . . .'

'That's a long time to live in limbo. Not divorced, not married either.'

Her head was beginning to ache. She put a hand to her temples. Stewart caught the movement, and must have read it correctly. 'I'm not trying to hurt you, Cathy,' he said. 'But we do have to talk. For your own sake as much as for mine.'

'You're right, I know that.'

'Has Jarrod been in touch with you at all?'

'Once I left the old flat he wouldn't have known where to find me.'

'Have you made an effort to see him?'

'No.'

She could have made the effort, but had not done so. For there had been a time, in those first two months after she had left Marakizi, when Jarrod could have found her. If their marriage had meant something to him, surely he'd have done so. Two months of hoping . . . Of tensing every time the 'phone rang. Of a sick breathlessness when the post was pushed under the door.

'No,' she said again now, her tone harder.

Wisely Stewart did not press her further. He seemed to understand that she needed some time alone to think, to make sense of her feelings, before she could accept the fact that her marriage to Jarrod was over.

They would talk the next day he said and kissed her lightly. Cathy watched through the window as he drove away, then she found Mrs Fairchild, told her she had done as much as she could that day, and left the house too. Her headache had grown worse and she needed an alert mind in order to decide on colour schemes and design.

She went back to the office, learned there was nothing urgent needing her attention, and then she drove to a quiet place that she had always enjoyed.

The Wilds were an oasis of peacefulness not far from the hub of the city. Rising from lush lawns rose a rugged kopje that was a rock-garden of indigenous flowers. Everywhere there was colour. Purple vygies sprawled over sunny rocks. Daisies grew in profusion, vivid yellow and white Barberton daisies, orange Namaqualand daisies, spreading over the ground like a carpet. Here and there proteas and aloes stood between the rocks. With their great waxen blooms they seemed to belong in this setting.

Twenty minutes of walking took Cathy to the top of the kopje. At its pinnacle was a sun-dial. Fingering the weathered surface, she traced the different lines to their compass points. She lingered on north-east. That way led to Marakizi. To Jarrod.

Which way to Canada? North too. North-west she supposed. Much further north than Marakizi. So very much further. A different continent. A different hemisphere.

Her eyes left the sun-dial and rested on the scenery beneath her. Spreading in all directions were the suburbs of Johannesburg, a great sprawl of green and lilac, for it was summer and the mauve-flowered jacarandas were in bloom. There would be no jacarandas in Canada. At this time of the year there would likely be lots of snow and ice.

There were no jacarandas at Marakizi either. In the experimental compound of the game-park there were mopanis and acacias and flame-trees. One special flame-tree. She had watched while Jarrod had dug the hole. And then she had placed the tree in the ground. And after that . . .

Dashing an angry hand at the tears that suddenly filled her eyes, she turned her gaze deliberately Canada-wards once more. It was time to stop thinking about Marakizi. About Jarrod. Time to face the fact that three years of love and passion and happiness were past.

Stewart was a good man. Warm and kind. Fun, too. Through their love of art, though it took different forms in their lives, they had something in common. She would find contentment with him. And it would not matter that she had once had much more than mere contentment in her life.

'I'm so glad,' Stewart said simply, the next evening, when she told him she would marry him.

'I still have to get divorced,' she reminded him.

'You've overcome the biggest hurdle. Acceptance of the inevitable. Will you 'phone Jarrod?'

'There is no 'phone at Marakizi.'

That had been one of the problems. Things might have turned out differently if there had been a telephone.

'I'll have to write to him,' she said.

'There isn't much time.'

'It's the only way to reach him.'

'Well all right then. It will take a while for the divorce to become final, but at least we'll know that it's just a question of waiting.'

A week passed without a reply from Jarrod. The post was slow, they would hear from him, Cathy assured Stewart, wishing she herself was convinced. Another week passed, and Stewart was no longer convinced either. He was beginning to get edgy.

'What's he playing at?' he demanded, pacing the floor of Cathy's small living-room.

'The post . . .'

'Doesn't take that long! There must be somewhere we could reach him by 'phone, Cathy.'

'The two lodges. But he won't be there, not at this time of the year.'

'They could get a message through to him.'

'They might not.'

They would, of course, but Jarrod would ignore it. Just as he had chosen to ignore the letter.

'Talk about the back of beyond.' Stewart's habitual good humour was beginning to wear thin. 'Doesn't your ex-husband believe in civilisation?'

The tone of the question irritated her. 'Marakizi is Jarrod's idea of civilisation. And he isn't an ex yet.'

Stewart looked at her tensely. 'Sorry about that. I didn't mean to catch you on the raw.'

'That's all right.' She was feeling remorseful herself. Stewart was the future. Jarrod didn't need defending, he had always coped very well on his own.

'Perhaps another day or two,' she attempted.

'You don't really believe that we'll hear from him, do you?' Stewart observed evenly.

After a long moment, Cathy said, 'No.'

Stewart stopped his pacing and threw her a harassed look. 'What do you suggest we do?'

'I may have to go to Marakizi.'

'No!'

'I'm beginning to think it's the only way.'

Stewart's eyes were stormy. 'I don't want you going back to that place.'

A pale face turned to his. 'Do you think *I* want it?' Cathy asked painfully.

He looked at her uncertainly, apparently taken aback by the emotion he saw in her face. In a moment he was beside her. 'I'm sorry, my darling. I didn't realise ... It will mean digging up unpleasant memories.'

'Not only unpleasant ones.' She looked at him steadily, wishing that she could quell the nervousness inside her. 'There are happy memories too.'

'Cathy ...'

'You have to understand that,' she said urgently. 'I was happy at Marakizi. Until that last day ...' She stopped, then met his eyes bravely. 'It was my home.'

'I wish you'd never met Jarrod.'

'But I did. I was married to him. You can't wipe out the past, Stewart, as if it had never happened.'

'You never talk about it,' he said, still uncertain.

'But it's there.' She put a hand on his arm. 'You'd be better off with someone else, someone ...'

'Don't say that!' he cut in fiercely, and she felt his muscles tense beneath her hand.

'A girl who was never married. Someone without a past.' She was thinking of Anna, a pretty blonde girl Stewart had dated now and then before he'd met Cathy.

'No.' He drew her to him, holding her with one

arm, sliding his hand beneath her hair to cradle her head against his chest with the other. 'It's you I want. Be patient with me, Cathy.'

'I will be,' she whispered.

He held her a little away from him then, so that he could look into her eyes. 'I wish I could have been the first. But I wasn't, and I accept it. You haven't been in touch with Jarrod for almost a year and that's good enough for me. So I'm not even going to ask if you're still in love with him.'

Which was just as well. For she would have found it impossible to answer the question. Everything that had happened notwithstanding.

'You really think it's necessary to go out to Marakizi?' Stewart asked at last.

'I'm afraid so.'

'Right then.' Spoken in the tone of one who had made a decision. 'When do we go?'

She drew back to look at him, her eyes wide and surprised. 'We?'

He grinned down at her. 'I'm coming with you, of course.'

'But Stewart . . . You have so much to do here.'

'The work will have to wait a day or two. You didn't think I would let you go on your own, did you?'

She hadn't thought of that aspect at all. Just the idea of going to Marakizi was enough to fill her head.

'It will make it easier for you if I'm there. You won't have to handle Jarrod on your own.'

'Jarrod isn't a man who takes easily to handling,' Cathy said, a little unsteadily.

Stewart gave her a searching look. He seemed about to say something, then to think better of it. After a few moments he suggested, 'Why don't we leave on Friday? That way we could be back Sunday at the latest.'

'Sounds okay.' She tried to inject a positive note into her tone.

Things were moving so fast. Too fast. Divorce and remarriage. A move to the other end of the world. A visit to Marakizi. Major events in her life, every one of them. Events needing time to get used to, to think through. Yet they were happening almost simultaneously, without any prior knowledge on her part that they were going to happen at all. For months her life had progressed on a more or less even keel, and all at once it was as if forces outside herself were hurtling her towards a destiny over which she had no control.

'Where is Marakizi anyway?' Stewart asked.

'I'll get a map and show you.'

She was about to slip away from him, glad of the few minutes it would take her to find the map, when his arms tightened around her, and he said, 'Later.'

'Later . . .?'

'I want to hold you, darling.'

He began to kiss her, and instinctively her lips closed against him. She was not ready for this. And then she felt the stiffening in his arms, and remembered that they were now engaged, and she wound her arms around his neck. As she forced herself to open her lips to his she hoped he did not know quite how hard she was trying.

They left very early on Friday morning. In the opaque light of dawn the city had a greyness which even the vivid colour of the jacarandas could not penetrate. As the sleeping suburbs were left behind them, the flat humps of the gold-mines loomed here and there out of the mist, for this was the Witwatersrand, the long reef of white waters, where the gold of the world was mined, with Johannesburg its industrial and financial heart.

The car sped easily along the tar. The gold-mines were left behind, and now they were surrounded by farm-land, endless miles of farm-land. Much of it was pathetically dry, for a terrible drought had taken its toll in Africa. 'If only it would rain,' Cathy said.

The further north they travelled, the more jittery Cathy became. She was relieved that Stewart was preoccupied, for she was in no mood for trivial chatter. In no condition for it. Her stomach was a tight churning knot of nerves, and her throat was dry.

After a while Stewart turned on the radio. The strains of a popular song filled the car, and Stewart whistled softly along with it. Cathy turned slightly in her seat to look at him. He was a nice-looking man. His features were clean-cut, his smile appealing. She was lucky to have met him Mrs Fairchild had said, upon learning of the engagement. And she *was* lucky she told herself now.

She was also glad that she had had a chance to live on her own for a while. She had proved to herself that she could be independent. That she could support herself, that she could meet crises head-on and work through them on her own. That she could deal with life by herself, without needing a man to turn to every time things became difficult.

But she had also learned something else about herself. By nature she was not a loner. She needed to be able to share her life with someone else. Comfortable as she was with her own company, there were occasions when she had felt the need of another person with whom to share an experience, if only to laugh together at a joke or to cry at something sad.

Nowhere was it carved in stone that she could love only one man in her lifetime. She tried to push aside the memory of her response to Stewart's kisses. She was not so naïve as not to know that she had been trying to prove something to herself as much as she'd felt the need to prove it to Stewart. If he'd sensed her difficulty he had not said so. Anyway, she resolved, it was a difficulty that she would overcome. She had been tired, overwrought with the knowledge that the meeting with Jarrod lay ahead. In Canada, alone with Stewart, things would be different.

And she tried to silence the little voice that told her that with Jarrod she had never had to put on an act. With Jarrod there had been a wild passion and excitement, a wonderful fulfilment. Too wonderful. The marriage had not lasted. Perhaps it had not been meant to last.

'Tell me about Jarrod,' Stewart said.

'You'll meet him soon.'

'Tell me anyway. I've always liked to know something about the competition. Helps one to approach a situation from a position of strength.'

There was something strangely grim in his tone, so that Cathy turned to look at him again. 'Jarrod isn't competition for you.'

Stewart took a hand from the wheel and covered one of Cathy's. 'Remember that when you see him again, will you?'

They had left the Highveld and were in the Lowveld now. They had been travelling some hours, and in that time the scenery had changed. The khaki-coloured scrub of the Highveld had given way to a lusher greenness, the flatness to rolling hills and mountains. At present they were travelling through timber country, and Cathy wound down her window and smelled the freshness of the air.

I've missed this, she thought. Oh, I've missed this so much.

Beside her, Stewart said, 'You've never talked about Jarrod.'

To continue in silence would make him even more suspicious than he was already.

After a moment she said, 'I didn't think it was important.'

'Either that,' Stewart countered levelly, 'or it was *too* important.'

Perceptive man. If Jarrod had not meant quite so much to her it would have been no effort to talk about him.

'He's an outdoor type,' she said quietly, preferring not to rise to Stewart's last words. 'Everything he does is linked to the outdoors. His business ventures, his own special interests. I couldn't see Jarrod being happy in a city.'

'Tell me about his businesses.'

'He owns two private game-lodges. Very fine ones. He built them from scratch so to speak. They're well-run, efficient, and people get what they come for—they see plenty of game. We've had tourists from all over the world.'

'We . . .' Stewart let the word lie between them.

'I'm sorry, I meant Jarrod.' Cathy pushed away the slight feeling of irritation.

'And then there's Marakizi,' she went on, and was unaware that her voice had changed.

'Why do I get the feeling that Marakizi is special?'

'Because it is,' she said on a rush of emotion. 'Marakizi is private, Stewart. No tourists are allowed there. It's our . . . It's Jarrod's home.'

This time he let the offending word go. 'Some sort of experimental station I think you once said?'

'That's right. For quite some time now Jarrod has been studying giraffe. Their habits, their life-span, what they eat, how they behave. Anything to do with giraffe.'

'Why?'

'Because it's what he loves to do,' Cathy said simply.

After a moment Stewart said, 'He must be a rich man.'

'A very rich man.'

'And yet he's content to bury himself in some lonely outpost studying giraffe.'

'You make it sound so ridiculous. As if he was some kind of eccentric. He's not that at all,' she said hotly.

'You're going to great lengths to defend him.'

'I'm not defending him,' she protested, and knew she was doing precisely that.

'I think you are.'

This was getting childish. Her chest tight with strain, she said, 'Let's not argue.'

'We're just talking, darling.'

'We *can't* let ourselves argue about Jarrod.'

'I just want to know about him,' Stewart said stubbornly.

'He belongs to the past.'

'I hope so.'

She thought he would leave the subject alone, but a mile further on he said, 'Even without having seen Marakizi, I can't seem to picture you there. You're a city person, Cathy. A competent interior-decorator. You enjoy galleries and night-life. What did you do with yourself in the bundu all day?'

'I helped Jarrod.'

She turned to him, taking in a profile that had acquired an unaccustomed hardness, and knew that whether he liked it or not there were certain things he had to accept.

'Jarrod hopes to write a book about giraffe some day. A kind of definitive study. I had my part in it.' A little muscle tightened in Stewart's jaw, but she went on notwithstanding. 'I did sketches. Hundreds of sketches. That was how I used my art. And photos. Stewart, I *enjoyed* it, don't you understand?'

'I understand that it may not have been a good idea to take you back there after all.'

'You're wrong,' she said in a low voice. 'Everything's changed. After ... well, after what happened I couldn't live there ever again. Couldn't be happy there.'

'Do you mean that?'

'Oh yes.' She slid across the seat and leaned her head against his shoulder. 'I can't pretend that part of my life never happened, but it's over. I want to be with *you*, Stewart. Only with you now.'

'I suppose we had no option but to come here.' He sounded somewhat reassured. 'It wasn't really your choice to come to Marakizi. Nor mine.'

The choice had been Jarrod's. Cathy had understood that from the beginning.

It was all so familiar. Every bend and turn of the road. The clump of mopanis before the little bridge. The acacias just there on the rise. A few yards further on would be a glade, and they would find impala grazing there, as they'd grazed there since time immemorial. Oh, and there was the windmill turning slowly in the breeze, the long blades glinting in the sun. Did the old wart-hog still come at sun-set to drink from the water-hole? Cathy wondered.

It was all just as she had remembered it. That was what struck her as she sat forward in her seat and took it all in. 'Nothing has changed,' she said once. But she kept back the words, 'I've come home.'

Because it wasn't home. Not any longer. Even discounting the fact that the words would have hurt Stewart immeasurably, she couldn't have said them. It was *not* home. That was what she must keep reminding herself.

And then they drove up to the little fenced compound and she saw almost immediately that things had changed after all. The changes fairly leaped at her. There was a landing-strip where there had been none before, and on it stood a helicopter. There were telephone wires. A telephone! Heavens, had Jarrod had a brain-storm?

But there was no time to assimilate what she saw, for the car drew to a halt and a man walked out of the building that was the research lab.

'Jarrod?' Stewart asked tensely.

'Yes.'

He was coming towards them, a superbly built figure in a safari-suit. His gait was long and loose and somehow uncompromising. The rugged face was unsmiling. At his heels ran a dog.

'Tough customer,' Stewart muttered.

'I'm nervous,' Cathy said, and felt her heart thudding hard against her rib-cage.

'He can't hurt you.' Stewart gave her hand a quick squeeze.

Jarrod had reached the car by the time Cathy and Stewart had got out of it. Cathy's stomach muscles were so tight now that she thought she might faint from the pain. For a long moment no one spoke, and then Jarrod said softly, 'Welcome home.'

Trust him to catch her off balance, she thought bitterly, as she bent to rub her hand along the ruff of an ecstatic Jock. Jarrod's face had been totally devoid of surprise at sight of the car. He knew why she was here. Had known they were coming.

From behind her she heard Stewart's hissing intake of breath. The moment with the dog had given her time to control her features. She straightened now and Stewart put an arm around her shoulders. Deliberately Cathy took a step closer to him. She had been so determined that they would all be civilised. Jarrod, it seemed, had other ideas.

'It's not home any more,' she said, very calmly. And then, knowing the words should ordinarily have been spoken first, 'Hello, Jarrod.'

Time had wrought changes in Jarrod too. Surely his

face had not always been quite so stern, so strict? The lines around his mouth, those were new. And the strange look in his eyes—a haunted look. He was a man who laughed easily, but there was no laughter in him now. Despite the few moments with the dog, Cathy's legs felt weak, and the blood was pumping uncomfortably hard at the side of her throat. She had to get a grip on herself.

It was introduction time. 'Stewart, this is Jarrod. Jarrod, Stewart Robinson. My fiancé.'

They were among the hardest words she had ever uttered.

The expression on Jarrod's face did not change. He had indeed received her letter, for if he had not she would see his shock. He lifted an eyebrow in Stewart's direction and extended his hand. After a moment Stewart's hand went to meet it. Cathy watched the brief clasp, the one hand pale and smooth, the other tanned and long-fingered and hard.

'Well . . .' Stewart said a little inadequately, and stopped.

Cathy didn't blame him for his awkwardness. They could hardly go on standing there, on the sun-baked ground, looking at each other. It had been a mistake after all to come back to Marakizi. She should have written another letter to Jarrod. Should have insisted on a reply. No matter if the divorce had been dragged out a few weeks longer. Anything would have been better than this.

'You know why we're here,' she said, tension edging her face with sharpness. 'Jarrod, let's go and sit down. We can't talk like this.'

'Where's my child?' Jarrod asked.

Cathy drew a great shuddering breath. Now, when she needed it most, her control seemed to be deserting her. The blood drained from her cheeks as she stared at him.

'You haven't brought the baby with you?'

She couldn't answer him. She made a little futile gesture with her hand, then dropped it. On the periphery of her consciousness she felt Stewart's hand tighten on her shoulder, giving her support.

'I suppose you thought I wouldn't be interested,' Jarrod said in a hard tone.

'It's not ... It's ...'

'Well?' he demanded.

'I think I should leave you both to talk alone,' Stewart said tactfully.

She swung round. 'No, please ...'

'Yes, my darling.' He held her against him a moment, as if to give her some of his strength. 'This is between you and Jarrod.'

'Stewart ...'

'I'll take a walk along the fence. I'll be there when you want me.'

I want you now. I *need* you. I don't think I can face Jarrod alone.

'Well, Cathy?'

She forced herself to meet Jarrod's gaze. His eyes were narrowed, his mouth tight. She swallowed. 'We can't talk here.'

'Okay,' he said crisply. 'We'll go to our bungalow.'

Our ... As Stewart had done earlier, she let the word go. Never mind that Jarrod had used it deliberately to shock her, or to hurt her. She felt so shattered that she knew she could only deal with one issue at a time.

Not a word passed between them as they made their way to the round white-washed bungalow with the honey-suckle tumbling over the walls. Two stony-faced people, too acutely aware of each other to make small-talk in the way of complete strangers.

The door was open. Cathy walked in ahead of Jarrod, aware of him close behind her—so aware that the hairs pricked the back of her head—and she stepped quickly away from him as she came inside.

'This has changed too,' she said, struck by the clinical look of the place.

'Nothing's changed,' he said briefly.

'It looks so spartan.' For a moment she wondered why. The furniture was the same. The pictures. Nothing had been added or removed. 'It looks different without all my clutter,' she said after a moment, and it didn't need the tightening of his lips to know that she had said the wrong thing.

'My untidiness always did irritate you,' she hurried on too quickly. 'And there are other changes. I saw the landing-strip as we came in.'

'The baby,' Jarrod cut in.

'And the telephone wires.'

'Stop this Cathy! Where is the baby?'

She did stop then. She was behaving stupidly. But somehow it had never occurred to her that he didn't know . . .

In a voice so low as to be barely audible, she said, 'There is no baby, Jarrod.'

CHAPTER TWO

'WHAT!'

He looked shaken. Beneath his tan his face was suddenly pale. Watching him, Cathy felt unsuspected pity wrenching inside her.

'What happened?' She heard the choking sound in his voice.

'It was born dead.'

'Oh, Cathy. Cathy, darling.'

In that moment there was no Stewart. No thought of divorce. There was just Jarrod. White and shocked and more vulnerable than she had ever seen him.

Cathy took a step towards him. She put her hand on his arm as he muttered again, 'What happened?'

'Broken placenta. Not enough oxygen. The baby just died.'

'And you never let me know,' he said brokenly.

The words brought memory flooding back. Dropping her hand, she stepped away from him. From a face that was as white as his, she looked at him angrily.

'You should have been here.'

'Why didn't you let me know, Cathy? And why did you go away?'

'You should have been here. Don't you understand?' There was hostility in her voice now. 'It needn't have happened, Jarrod.'

'You're blaming me?'

'Yes!' The pity she had felt moments ago was gone. 'You should have been here at Marakizi when I went into labour. Things went wrong from the start. I had to get to the hospital.' She stopped. 'Oh, what's the use . . . It's water under the bridge by now.'

'I want to know.' He was still pale, and his body had a rigid look, but his voice had regained some semblance of control.

'You speak as if it's your right.'

'It is. I was the father.'

'Who didn't care enough to be around when he was needed.'

He flinched. The words had hurt, but she was past caring. She had been so terribly hurt herself.

'Remember the day you went off without me?' she asked.

'Of course.'

'I wasn't feeling well.'

'The baby wasn't due yet.'

'So we thought. The labour started soon after you left.'

Something flickered in the eyes that never left her face. An expression that was akin to pain. Well, it was right that Jarrod should feel some sense of remorse. Cathy stifled the pity that welled inside her again.

'I was desperate. Alone in the compound. No way of getting word to you. To the lodges. I began to have wild thoughts of having to deliver the baby myself!'

'My poor Cathy.' Once more there was the break in his voice.

'Your poor Cathy,' she mocked him. 'Pity you didn't think that way then. It was your choice to leave me here, Jarrod.'

'Yes . . .'

'Amos could have taken me to the hospital,' she said, thinking of the head-ranger, Jarrod's right-hand man in all matters. 'But he was with you. And Lena and Tinus had gone away too. It was a Sunday, remember?'

'But you did get to the hospital?'

'Some people arrived. Tourists. They'd lost their

way, and somehow ended up here. I asked them to help me. I was half crazy with fear by that time . . .'

She stopped. For almost a year now she had been trying to shut the memories from her mind. But they were all coming back to her now. Such painful memories.

She curled her nails hard into the palms of her hands. 'Their name was Anderson. They were very kind. They drove me to the hospital. The man was in a sweat, the woman had me stretched out on the back seat of the car. She talked to me all the time, tried to get me to relax.'

'Go on.'

'We got to the hospital. And the baby was born. But it had been deprived of oxygen for too long.'

She did not tell him that it had been a little girl. Though Jarrod deserved to suffer, the additional information would have bordered on cruelty. He looked tormented enough at the knowledge that his child was dead.

'Are you saying—if you'd had help earlier it would have lived?'

The scene was still raw in Cathy's mind. The weary doctor, angered at the unnecessary loss of a life, saying, 'You should have come earlier. Don't wait so long next time.'

Next time . . . There would be no next time. At least not in this particular corner of the world. If Cathy had more babies they would be born in Canada.

She looked at Jarrod, saw the tautness in his face, and felt anger do battle with compassion. 'It might have been different,' she said. 'I can't be positive.'

The skin on Jarrod's face was stretched so tight that it seemed almost as if it might snap. 'What happened afterwards?' he asked.

'I went back to Johannesburg.'

'Johannesburg! This was your home. Didn't you think about me, Cathy?'

'I couldn't return to Marakizi. I . . . I had to get away. Can you understand?' She paused, searching his eyes, and found herself unable to read them.

'I went to the flat,' she said.

'I see,' he said in an odd tone.

'You could have 'phoned me there any time. I kept waiting for you to 'phone.'

'You could have 'phoned too.'

'Marakizi didn't have a 'phone,' she pointed out with asperity.

'You could have left a message at one of the lodges. Why didn't you?'

'Because it was up to you to get hold of me.'

The eyes that flicked her face were hard. 'So you stood on your pride, did you?'

'Don't mock me, it doesn't impress me in the least.' She lifted her head defiantly. 'I waited, Jarrod.'

'For how long?'

'Two months. Two whole months. You could have found me. There were only a few places I could have been. It seems you didn't care enough even to try.'

It was very silent in the room. For a minute at least neither of them spoke. At length Cathy said, 'I begged you to stay with me that day. I begged you not to leave me.'

She looked at him, and saw that his expression had changed once more. It was almost as if Jarrod had detached himself from his surroundings.

'Why did you go?' she demanded. 'It would have been so easy for you to stay.'

'You don't know that.'

'What was it? Some urgent piece of information on one of the transmitters that couldn't have waited? Something more important than the birth of a baby?'

'Stop this,' he ordered.

'Oh no, Jarrod, I'll say what I please. I've waited a

year to say it. It was your selfishness that took you away from me when I needed you most.'

'I told you to stop.'

'Selfishness,' she went on unheedingly. 'Unwillingness to put me first. You didn't believe I could be in labour.'

'You weren't due yet,' he pointed out.

'Babies have been known to arrive early. What was so important that day anyway?'

As if he had not heard the question—or did not deem it worth answering—Jarrod walked to the window. Cathy watched him. He stood looking out, his neck and shoulders rigid. Again Cathy felt compassion stirring unwanted inside her. This was not easy for him, she knew that. Not easy for any man to accept that but for him a baby would be alive. A part of her wanted to go to him, to touch him, to put her arms around him. They would weep together, and in their mutual grief and caring each would find some measure of comfort. She almost did go to him.

But another part of her kept her standing by the door. It tore her apart to see Jarrod suffer like this. In the light of what had happened it hurt more than she would have expected. But she could not go to him. In time he would get over the shock. He would learn to live with it. Just as she had. But she could not help him do it. The time for that had long passed.

'I did try the flat,' he said at length.

She suppressed a gasp. 'You did? Jarrod, when?'

He swung round. 'March it would have been.'

'March! I was gone by then.' She gave a hard laugh. 'My God, Jarrod, how long did you think I'd wait around for you? By March I was starting to make a new life for myself.'

'Meaning?' His voice was hard too now. It did not take Jarrod long to compose himself, she thought.

'Meaning that I'd gone back to interior-decorating.

Remember I had almost finished my training when I met you? Well, I did the exam. I found a job. And a new flat.'

'A new image too.' His eyes were on her, studying her. 'City clothes. A city hairstyle.'

'Don't sneer,' she said tightly. 'You don't have the right to look down on me.'

'And you also found yourself a boyfriend.' There was contempt in his expression.

She nodded, resenting his attitude, but determined to play this scene coolly. 'Stewart *was* a boyfriend. He's now my fiancé.'

In a second Jarrod had crossed the room. His eyes were stony, his jaw a long cruel line as he seized her wrist. 'Not a fiancé, Cathy. You're married.'

'Not for much longer.' Her heart was pounding wildly but her raised chin and level gaze presented at least an outward show of composure. 'Why didn't you answer the letter? And let go my hand.'

'It bothers you so much to have me touch you?' he asked softly.

Despite the deliberate seductiveness of his tone, there was nothing even remotely lover-like in his touch. And yet as his fingers burned on her skin, ripples of response shivered through her system. Will I never be free of you, Jarrod? she wondered on a little wave of despair.

'Yes, it bothers me.'

'It never used to.'

'Stewart wouldn't like it,' she said flatly.

'Of course, we should be considering Stewart,' he jeered.

'Let's not play games, Jarrod. Why didn't you answer the letter?'

A thumb stroked the delicate area just above her wrist, and Cathy had to steel herself to remain very still. This was another game, a deadlier game, for

Jarrod knew what he was doing to her. He had always known.

His hand dropped away from her, and he said, 'I chose not to.'

'I want a divorce, Jarrod.'

'So you said in the letter.'

'I want it quickly.'

'Why?'

'Stewart is an architect, he's been offered an excellent job in Canada.'

'And he wants you to go with him.'

'Yes.' It should have been easy to meet the level gaze of dark brown eyes, but it was not easy at all.

'Had you thought of going as his mistress?'

Cathy suppressed a desire to scream. 'I'm going as his wife. But I told you all that in my letter.'

'So you did. Why Stewart?'

'Don't put me though this, Jarrod,' she said, a little hysterically.

'I'll do what I damn well like, my darling,' he responded, his tone never changing. 'Why Stewart? He's not your type.'

'Let that be my concern. All I ask is a divorce.'

'Such a little thing.'

'We don't want to be married to each other any longer.'

He pushed his hands into the pockets of his trousers. 'I don't remember that we ever discussed it.'

'It's obvious. You weren't there when I needed you most. It was a few months before you made any effort to contact me.'

There was silence in the room. Strange, Cathy thought, silence had always been present in their marriage. The silence of companionship. Silence when they read or worked in the same room. Silence when they drove together through the veld. The silence of tranquillity, at sunset, when they sipped a drink and gazed across the brooding veld. A shared silence that transcended the need for words, because each knew without words what the other was thinking and feeling.

The silence in the room now was altogether different. It was the silence of two wary, hostile people, each waiting for the other to make an offensive move.

'You could have got in touch with *me*,' Jarrod said at length, and his voice was odd.

'Oh no!' came the swift rejoinder. 'It was up to you. After what happened ... My God, Jarrod, have you no feelings at all? Don't you realise that the very last thing I would have done was get in touch with you?'

An eyebrow lifted slightly. 'Pride again.'

'If you want to call it that. Stewart must be wondering what's taking us so long. Are you going to give me the divorce?'

'Divorces aren't given in seconds, you know that Cathy. I doubt if you'd even have grounds for one.'

'I've thought of that ...' She bit her lip. 'But it could be arranged. All I ask is that you co-operate. Set me free, Jarrod.'

'That's what you really want?'

She injected some measure of enthusiasm into her voice. 'Yes.'

'You want my consent to a divorce?'

'Yes!'

This isn't happening, said a painful inner voice. Jarrod and I parting. Once we made promises. We were going to be together forever. Oh Jarrod, what happened to us?

'You'll get it,' he said briefly.

'Thank you.' She tried to sound pleased. 'I'll go and tell Stewart. You can give us some kind of letter for the lawyers—I'm not sure what they'd want, but it will get things moving—and then we'll be off.' She paused, and looked at him awkwardly. 'Jarrod ...

Jarrod, I suppose this is goodbye.' The words came out in a voice that was suddenly cracked.

'Not quite yet,' he said evenly.

'What do you mean?'

'I said you'd get my consent. I didn't say I'd give it today.'

She stared at him uncomprehendingly. 'What are you trying to say?'

'You won't get the consent today.'

'One moment you say you'll give it, and the next moment you say you won't.' She made a little gesture of helplessness. 'What are you playing at?'

'I said I'd give you my consent,' he said crisply. 'And I will. A week from now.'

A little quiver of apprehension began to creep along her spine. 'You'll send it to us in Johannesburg?'

'I'll give it to you right here at Marakizi.'

Cathy grew very still. He couldn't mean what he thought she meant. Aloud, as steadily as she was able, she said, 'So you want us to return to Johannesburg, and then drive back again a week later?'

'You will stay at Marakizi.'

He did mean it. He was leaning against the wall, one long leg stretched across the other. The rigidity had left him now. His face looked more relaxed. But it was a deceptive expression, Cathy knew. She saw the dark eyes, alert and perceptive, the slight tightness at the lips that perhaps only she, knowing him as well as she did, would discern. There was steel in that expression. In this mood Jarrod would be a difficult man to argue with.

She felt suddenly sick. There was to be no letting up as far as Jarrod was concerned. He would give her what she wanted, but she would have to pay for it.

Strange, she thought, she had never taken Jarrod for a vengeful man. Perhaps he'd changed. So much had changed.

'Jarrod, why?'

He shrugged. 'My reasons are my own.'

'We ... Stewart and I ... we can't stay here a week.'

'Tough.'

'We have to get back. There's so much to do before Stewart goes.'

'Stay here by yourself then.'

'I'm busy decorating a house.'

'Tough,' he said again.

She was getting nowhere with him. It was hard to believe that this was Jarrod, the man she had loved more than life itself. The man with whom she had lived and laughed and worked for three years.

Taking a step towards him, she tried a smile. 'Aren't you being a little unreasonable? It would be inconvenient for us to stay on here.'

'Then forget the divorce.'

'No!'

Something moved in his jaw. 'You have my terms.'

It was Cathy's turn to be silent. Warily she looked at him. He was lithe as a panther in his fawn safari-suit. And handsome. So handsome. After all this time he was still the most handsome man she knew, the most sexually attractive person she had ever met, was ever likely to meet. But happiness and harmony were not founded on sexual attraction, that much she had learned to her cost.

'Why are you doing this to us?' she asked at last.

'I choose to.'

'Just as you chose not to answer my letter.'

He inclined the glossy dark head. 'Precisely.'

Tears came into her eyes, she couldn't prevent them. 'To see me suffer, Jarrod, is that it?'

If her emotion touched him there was nothing to show it. 'You think I didn't suffer?' He spoke in a voice stripped of everything but anger. 'You know nothing of what I went through. You're not even interested. It was your choice to leave here, my darling wife. Your choice to come back. With your so-called fiancé. With your demands.'

She looked down at her tightly clenched hands. 'I wish you wouldn't see it that way.'

'Don't be a child. You don't set all the terms, Cathy. You will get the consent you want. But you will stay here a week. Take it or leave it.'

Jarrod could be a hard man, though till now she had never been the butt of his hardness. He wouldn't change his mind.

But she had to try. Though she was trying very hard to remain controlled, her voice trembled. 'It will be an ordeal for me, don't you realise that?'

'I don't give a damn.'

'What's happened to you, Jarrod? I don't remember you being like this.'

His eyes glittered. 'Perhaps there was no reason.'

'You know how much Marakizi means to me. Doesn't it matter to you that I'll be hurting all the time?'

The line of his mouth was inflexible. 'You talk about hurting. You suffered, Cathy, and I'm deeply sorry about the baby, you have to believe that. But I suffered too.'

He hadn't answered the question. He didn't need to. Cathy understood that he blamed for her leaving Marakizi, for staying away when she should have come back. And when she had come back it was with another man. Seeing her hurt must be Jarrod's way of exacting punishment.

There was something dark and dangerous about him. The powerful build. The tension in his body. A predator holding himself in control, yet ready to leap on his prey when it suited him.

She had never been frightened of him. But she was

frightened now. And in a strange way she was also wildly excited. This was the thing Stewart could not do, he could not stir such extreme emotions in her. Only Jarrod could do that.

'We were so happy,' she said, giving it one more try. 'Does it have to end like this, Jarrod? With hostility? With suffering?'

'You want a quick civilised end, do you?' His eyes were on her lips, moving insolently to her throat, to breasts that he had carressed night after night in love and in passion.

'Yes.' Her throat was suddenly very dry. 'Change your mind, Jarrod, please.'

'It seems I'm not a civilised man, by your definition at least. No, Cathy, my way, or not at all.' He spoke succinctly. 'Well, what's your answer?'

'I don't think I have a choice,' she said wearily. 'Seems we'll have to stay.' She turned to the door. 'I'll go and talk to Stewart.'

'Not so fast.'

She turned back. 'What now?'

'There's the small matter of sleeping-arrangements.'

She met his eyes. 'I don't think there's much to discuss. You and I don't share a room any more.'

He came away from the window and took a few steps towards her, walking with a deliberation that set her pulses racing. 'I was talking about you and Stewart. One room or two?'

'Two,' she said, without thinking.

'So,' he said, sounding amused, 'you don't sleep together. Keeping him waiting till you're married, are you?'

'Just observing the proprieties while we're at Marakizi,' she lied, and looked away.

'I'd insist on having you in my bed if I were Stewart.'

From beneath her lashes she saw the gleam in his

eyes, and the way his lips lifted to reveal strong white teeth. They were on sexual ground now and it seemed to bring out the devil in Jarrod. Something primeval stirred in Cathy, and she knew she had to fight it. 'You always were a single-minded man,' she got out.

'I'd like you in my bed now,' he said, and his eyes moved over her body. 'What about it?'

It was very hard to maintain an outer coolness when her senses leaped at the outrageous suggestion. 'I won't lower myself with an answer,' she said stiffly.

'You don't have to.' He laughed seductively. 'There's a little pulse beating at the base of your throat that says it all for you.' A finger snaked out suddenly, touched the pulse oh so lightly, made it beat even faster than before.

Jarrod laughed again. 'You see, my darling, I know you so well. You say I'm single-minded. By which you mean that I like to make love to you. It's what you like too.'

'I used to,' she said very steadily.

'A week of separate rooms, Cathy? You're a passionate woman. You'll be climbing the walls with frustration.'

The blood was pounding in her ears. 'You really are uncivilised.'

'Shall I show you just how uncivilised I am?'

In a moment he had closed the gap between them, moving so quickly that she could not have got through the door if she'd tried. His arms closed around her body with the ease of familiarity. She twisted her body and tried to get away, but Jarrod held her so tightly that she could not free herself.

'Jarrod, no, please no,' she whispered, tilting her head so that she could look at him.

'You're appealing to an uncivilised man. You must know that's futile,' he grinned.

He bent his dark head, and his lips touched her throat, brushing, burning the soft skin. Cathy's involuntary cry was half pain, half pleasure. She had forgotten quite how sensuous Jarrod could be.

And then he began to kiss her, and she no longer tried to push him away because all her self-will was gone. There was just the crazy beat of her heart, and the desire that flooded her loins, and the wish, the quite appalling wish, that this moment could go on forever. As his kisses deepened, becoming hungrier, more possessive, she opened her lips to him, and then she put her arms around his neck. The time apart had not lessened the effect Jarrod had on her. She was only just hanging on to the barest thread of control.

His hands were at her back, pushing up her shirt, sliding on to the warm bare skin, and she gave another moan of pleasure. She'd dreamed of Jarrod. Dreamed that he was making love to her. Had never thought it would happen again.

And then he was lifting her against him, so that her feet left the floor, and he was carrying her across the room.

'Where are you taking me?' she managed to get out when he lifted his head to draw breath.

'To bed my darling, where else?'

The words brought back some sanity. She stared at him in horror, and she pushed her hands against his chest.

'No, Jarrod, no!'

'Don't be a fool, Cathy. Don't throw this chance away.'

'Stewart is out there, he's waiting for me.'

'He'll never know. It's as good as ever, Cathy, you know that.'

Once more she saw the wicked look in his eyes, the devilish lifting of his lips. And then she knew that he had planned this, that she had fallen right into his trap.

'You're disgusting!' she spat at him. 'Let me go!'

He did so without protest. Dumped her on the ground. Dropped his arms from her body.

'You're disgusting,' she said again.

'We must have something in common,' he said softly, dark eyes holding hers, defying them to move away. 'You were responding every bit of the way.'

'Force of habit,' she defended herself.

'Tell that to Stewart.' Jarrod gave an amused laugh. 'He might think you're not quite the right wife for him after all.'

'That's what it's all about, isn't it?' she flung at him. 'You don't want me. You made that clear a long time ago. But you don't like the thought of Stewart having me instead.'

He did not answer. His face was taut, mask-like. Only the eyes, hooded now and watchful, seemed alive.

'You're a swine,' Cathy said bitterly, over the pain in her throat. 'Thanks for opening my eyes, Jarrod. I'll be on my guard against you from now on.'

She was making for the door, when Jarrod spoke. 'Going back to Stewart in that state?'

She stopped in mid-step. God, what had she been thinking of!

'I'll have to use the bathroom,' she said stiffly.

'Through the bedroom,' he said politely.

'I still know the way.'

Pushing past him, she walked into the room that had been hers for three years. She would not look around, she promised herself. And found it was impossible not to.

Against her will, her eyes were drawn to the big double bed that took up much of the room. The same spread lay over it. At one end a tassleel was missing from the fringe. She remembered the day she and Jarrod had made love, laughing and in a hurry after a marvellous day in the veld. In such a hurry that they'd neglected to remove the spread. Jarrod had been kissing her, and they'd fallen backwards on to the bed, and the heel of her shoe had caught in the fringe, tearing the tassel. She'd meant to do some repairs.

Footsteps sounded behind her. Jarrod had come into the room. She saw that he'd registered the direction of her eyes.

'I never did get round to fixing that tassel,' she said, a little breathlessly.

'Not too late,' he said impassively.

'Wrong.' The word came out on a harder note. 'You're not helpless, Jarrod. Get yourself a needle and cotton.'

Quickly now, without waiting to see his reaction, she went into the bathroom.

Quite a sight greeted her in the mirror. Tousled hair, flushed cheeks and bruised lips. All of which could be repaired to some extent. But there were the eyes. What could she do about those? They were the eyes of a woman who had been making love.

Her limbs were trembling and her breath was coming in long shuddering gasps. She had to calm down. She could not let Stewart see her in this state. It was not as if she was some innocent virgin who had been roused to sudden passion. Jarrod had kissed her, that was all that had happened—even if it felt like so much more.

Damn you, Jarrod! Oh damn you! she said silently as she found a comb and raked it through her hair before splashing her face with cold water.

Her breathing began to slow and she was able to think again. The next week would be an ordeal. Jarrod would do nothing to make it easier for her, that much she now knew. But if he hoped to upset her he would be frustrated. She was prepared now. He would not have things all his own way.

CHAPTER THREE

JARROD was not in the room when she emerged from the bathroom. With her appearance somewhat restored she walked out of the bungalow and into the sun.

Stewart was no longer at the fence. She walked a little way, and found him in the shade of some mopani trees. He looked a little dispirited, but he brightened when he saw her.

'This heat!' he exclaimed. 'Don't you find it exhausting?'

Refraining from telling him that she loved it, Cathy said tactfully, 'It can be tough when you're not used to it. See any game, Stewart?'

'A few buck, that's all.'

'It's quiet in the veld at midday.' She was talking brightly, postponing the moment when she would have to talk about what had happened.

'How did things go with Jarrod?'

'Oh . . . fine.' At Stewart's sharp look she realised that the words had not come out quite right.

'Rough, honey?' he asked sympathetically.

'A little.'

He reached out a hand to touch a damp curl. 'More than a little I'd say. You look shaken.'

Stewart was nice. So very nice. She put her hand over his, taking pleasure from the comfort it gave her. Holding it between her cheek and her palm, she wondered how two men could be so different. A few minutes in Jarrod's company had been enough to stir her emotions, creating havoc in body and spirit. With Jarrod there was none of the calm peacefulness that she experienced when she was with Stewart.

She tried to ignore the little voice that reminded her that she was just twenty-three, and that there were other things in life to be enjoyed besides calm and peace, no matter how desirable those qualities might be.

'It wasn't easy,' she admitted unsteadily.

'He didn't seem to know about the baby.'

'No. That was a shock. I'd just assumed he knew. I don't know why . . .'

'You'd hardly have left him if there'd been a baby to hold you together.'

'Oh yes, I think I would have.' Cathy's voice was suddenly hard. 'After what happened . . . Jarrod's indifference. I wouldn't have stayed.'

Stewart was silent a moment, as if assessing her change of mood. Then he said, 'You discussed the divorce?'

'Of course.'

'He'll give his consent?'

'Yes,' Cathy said, a little lifelessly. 'He'll give it.'

'Wonderful.' Stewart gave her a hug. 'Let's get things signed and settled, then we can be off.'

'Stewart . . .'

'We could hit the highway long before dark, then drive straight through to Johannesburg.'

'No.' She pushed herself a little away from him. 'We can't leave here today.'

'Why not?'

'We have to stay a week.'

'Stewart looked first stunned, then appalled. 'That's impossible.'

'That's what I told Jarrod.'

'It doesn't take a week to give his consent.'

'He won't give it to us unless we stay the week.'

'That's blackmail!' Stewart exploded.

'Yes, it is.'

'We can get around it.'

Cathy looked at him levelly. 'How?'

'I'm not a lawyer, but I don't think he can do this. It's archaic. There must be ways to get around this.'

'Perhaps there are, I wouldn't know, but they would take more than a week to achieve. He's got us, Stewart. We stay at Marakizi a week and get his consent. Or we go, and seek other options. All of which would take very much longer. Even with the consent it will take time.'

'It will be something to start with. The man's holding a bloody gun to our heads.' Stewart's normally placid face was a study in frustration. 'I've work to do back home.'

Cathy remained silent. There was nothing to say. Stewart would have to come to terms with this. Just as she must do. Except that for her it would be more difficult.

'Are you saying we have no other options?' Stewart asked at last.

'I'm afraid so.'

'I'll have to 'phone Doug Jansen. Tell him I'll be delayed.

'Yes . . .'

'Why, honey, why? He must have a reason.'

'He has.'

'He thinks you'll come back to him.' Stewart spoke with sudden suspicion.

'Oh, no. He knows I won't do that.'

'Perhaps he thinks a week in his company will change your mind.'

'It's not that.' Cathy's throat felt raw. 'There was a time when . . . But . . . No, Stewart, Jarrod doesn't want me. You didn't see his eyes, the way he looked at me. The . . . the contempt.'

'Then why?'

Cathy released Stewart's hand and took a few steps

away from him. From where she stood she could see for miles across the veld. It was silent, brooding. A heat-haze shimmered over a kopje, the dazzle of the sun turning the sheer black rock surfaces to shining metal. To the naked eye no animals were visible, but they were there, she knew, motionless in whatever shade they could find, grateful of the temporary respite from danger, for in this heat no predator would attack.

Predator. Her mind went back to Jarrod. She had never thought of her husband as a predator. Ruthless, dangerous, waiting for the moment to attack. Was it only an over-active imagination that made her think of him that way now?

She knew that she had not answered Stewart's question, that he must wonder why. Turning her head just far enough so that he could hear her, she said, 'I gather that Jarrod was very upset when I went away. I think this is his revenge.'

'Bastard.' Stewart stared moodily into the distance.

Cathy shrugged. After the emotionally charged encounter with Jarrod she felt too fragile to pass comment on her husband. Later, when her heart-beats had settled back to normal, she might be able to think more rationally, might even be able to talk about Jarrod with Stewart. But not now.

'A week in this God-forsaken place,' Stewart muttered. 'What on earth will we do to pass the time?'

Cathy felt hysterical laughter bubbling in her throat. 'Drive around. See some game. People come a long way to do that.'

He eyed her narrowly. 'You're overwrought.'

It was an effort to stifle the laugh. 'What makes you say so?'

'You're not yourself.' He came to her and put his arms around her. Instinctively she stiffened. A few minutes ago, when she'd held his hand against her cheek, she'd been conscious of comfort. Now she felt repelled.

'Don't push me away,' Stewart said.

'I'm sorry.' She was contrite. 'You're right, I am overwrought.'

And inside her brain a desperate voice said, will it always be like this? This revulsion when Stewart touches me? When any man touches me? Will there always be the memory of Jarrod? The hunger for Jarrod?

'He made a pass at you, didn't he?' Stewart asked sharply.

So unexpected was the remark, and so astute, that Cathy flinched.

'He tried to make love to you?'

She looked at him helplessly, unable to answer.

'Well?' Stewart demanded.

'Yes,' she admitted after a moment.

'And you? Did you let him?'

This was too much. First Jarrod subjecting her to an ordeal, now Stewart.

'Don't you trust me?' she countered vehemently. 'My God, Stewart, the only reason we're here is because I want a divorce.'

'I just thought that maybe . . .'

'That maybe we'd slept together for old times' sake.' She was indeed overwrought now, and later she would understand that this was the reason she over-reacted. That and guilt, because Stewart was so close to the truth.

'You're going to be my husband,' she said. 'I don't want Jarrod. I can't stand the sight of him. I don't even want . . .'

She couldn't finish the sentence. Putting her hands over her eyes she shut back the tears that threatened to fall.

Stewart's arms closed around her again, and this

time she did not push him away. 'I'm sorry, darling, I'm so sorry,' he was saying. 'I shouldn't have doubted you. Cathy, don't cry. Please don't cry.'

They walked together through the compound, keeping to the shade. Cathy had regained some measure of outward control, and she told Stewart a little about Jarrod's work. She pointed out the orphanage, where orphaned animal babies were looked after until they were deemed able to look after themselves in the veld. The laboratory were Jarrod conducted his research. The guest-house where visiting scientists and zoologists slept when they visited Marakizi. Where she and Stewart would be put up, in their two separate rooms. Her voice was calm and matter-of-fact, hiding the anguish she felt as she walked around the place that was more 'home' than anywhere on earth. And she wondered whether some day she would feel this sense of belonging in Canada.

Let it happen soon, she prayed.

Word had spread that she was at Marakizi, and the staff came to say hello to her. Lena, the shy young girl who did house-keeping duties, and Tinus, who was being trained by Amos to be a ranger. Their beaming smiles revealed how happy they were to see Cathy, while side-long glances of curiosity were thrown quickly, fleetingly, to the man at her side.

Thus far Cathy had not seen Amos. The head-ranger was Jarrod's right-hand man. Having spent most of his life within a thirty-mile radius of Marakizi, what Amos did not know about the bushveld and about the animals which inhabited it was not worth knowing. Cathy supposed that he was out in the veld somewhere, gleaning information Jarrod needed for his research work.

They had gone almost once round the compound when they saw Jarrod emerge from the lab. Cathy felt her stomach muscles tauten as she watched him walking towards them. As always he gave the impression of a man who wielded power over himself and over others, an easy effortless power so that men—and women—responded quite naturally to his wishes. Except for herself, Cathy thought grimly. Oh, she had responded to him once, willingly, with abandon, because she loved him more than she had thought it possible to love a man. But things had changed. In the past year she had hardened herself, had determined that she would never again be in any man's power, for she never wanted to be hurt again as Jarrod had hurt her. If she gave—as she would with Stewart—it would be because that was what she wanted to do.

Jarrod had stipulated that she and Stewart stay a week at Marakizi, and they would do so. But she would not make things easy for him. Jarrod, she thought, wanted to see her suffer—and suffer she might—but she would try not to let him know it. She would not give him the satisfaction.

As he came nearer, she saw the arrogant line of the jaw, the clear intelligent eyes in the rugged face. He must have been working in the lab since their encounter in their—in *his* bungalow. Damn him, she thought again, on a fresh burst of anger. For a while he had seemed as shaken as she was. The news that their baby had been born dead had shocked him.

And yet he had been able to go from her to the lab, had probably worked with all his usual enthusiasm, just as if he had never been saddened, as if nothing had happened. Even the fact that he had kissed her for the first time in almost a year had not put him off his stride.

Was our lovemaking never more than a physical act? she wondered now. Was that all it ever meant to you, Jarrod? And why didn't I realise it?

At least the half hour away from him had given her time to compose herself. Thank goodness nobody had seen her with Stewart in the shade of the mopani trees. Jarrod would never know how he had affected her, how close she had come to crying.

'Time for lunch,' Jarrod said. 'You'll join me, of course.'

'Of course,' Cathy said bitterly, 'seeing we have no food of our own.'

'Cathy tells me you expect us to stay here a week,' Stewart blustered in a tone that Cathy had never heard him use before.

'Right. This way to the patio. That's where we'll be eating.'

Casting a glance at Stewart, Cathy saw that he was taken aback by Jarrod's easy handling of the subject. 'We can discuss it over lunch,' he said, after a moment.

Jarrod treated him to a friendly but entirely impersonal smile. 'Is there anything *to* discuss?'

Cathy held her breath, wondering how Stewart would react to what in any other man would have amounted to unforgivable rudeness. He opened his mouth, only to close it again. But as he fell into step behind Jarrod, he linked his arm through Cathy's, and she could feel the tension in the muscles that stretched from shoulder to hand.

Lunch was light and delicious, and Jarrod was an accomplished host. Whatever his game, Cathy thought, he was playing it expertly. She watched fascinated as Stewart, his anger notwithstanding, began to relax just a little.

Oh, but Jarrod was a master at charming people. She had seen it so often, men, women, listening to him, responding to him, mesmerised by the sheer force of his personality. Just as she had been mesmerised in those whirlwind days of their courtship.

Jarrod ignored her as he concentrated on Stewart, asking him questions about his work, about the move to Canada, appearing interested in every word that Stewart uttered. Cathy watched the tension begin to vanish from Stewart's face. Maestro, she thought grimly, and yet with a grudging admiration. Jarrod the maestro. Resentful though she was, she had to hand it to him—Jarrod would be able to relax a hissing viper if he so chose. He had a way with people. It was a way in which hollow flattery and compliments had no part—which made it all the more potent. His manner was so effortless, so very much a part of him. And today was the first time she had ever thought to question whether it was deliberate or not.

'I'm taking the jeep out into the veld,' he said when they had finished eating. 'Like to come along?'

'Sure, why not,' Cathy said, before Stewart could answer. She did not want to go with Jarrod, but refusing the offer, as Stewart might have done, would be making too big a deal of it. A case of protesting too much.

'We could go, I suppose.' Stewart looked uncertain.

Cathy found herself meeting the cool mocking depths of Jarrod's eyes. He knew what had prompted her decision—Jarrod, who had always known her almost as well as she knew herself. He knew just how much it would cost her to see the bushveld that was Marakizi again, knowing that it would be for the last time. He knew too that she could not stand the thought of seeing it in his company.

Her breathing was suddenly shallow. This would never do. Forcing a bright smile she looked at Stewart. 'Not much else to do around here.'

They set out twenty minutes later, the three of them in the front seat of the jeep. Cathy hadn't wanted to sit in the middle. She had stood back, hoping Stewart would get in first. But gallantly he had insisted on observing a lady's privileges.

He must know that sitting so close to her husband would bring responses and memories. He couldn't be so naïve as to believe otherwise. But perhaps Stewart was unconcerned. Perhaps he felt so secure in the knowledge that she had come here only to divorce Jarrod that he didn't care. Or perhaps, and the thought hit her with a slight shock, he was proving something to her. Forcing her to lay all her ghosts before she married him.

More fool he was if that was his reasoning. As she sat wedged tightly between the two men, it was Jarrod's thighs that drew her eyes, like powerful magnets, defying them to stray elsewhere. Jarrod's thighs which burned through her jeans, sending ripples of sensation along her legs, to her groin and up her back. Stewart was as close to her as Jarrod, but he might not have existed for all the impact he made on her.

Her chest felt tight and her breathing was shallow, though she made every effort to let it sound regular. And then Jarrod's thigh moved against hers, quite deliberately, and the breath jerked in her throat.

Oh, she had been a fool to come back. Worse than a fool. She should have known the effect Jarrod would have on her. It had always been like this between them, an instant and acute awareness. Despite Jarrod's outward show of indifference she knew he was as aware of her as she was of him. The mutual physical attraction that was stronger than anything she had ever known, still existed.

But there had to be more to a relationship than a marvellous sex life. There had to be understanding and warmth and a mutual concern. Without these attributes a relationship would wither and die. As their relationship had died, hers and Jarrod's. Which was why she had to leave him.

And yet she had been a fool to come here all the same. She knew that as she stole a quick sidelong glance at the strong profile, at the tanned muscular arms that held the wheel with such ease. She was not yet ready to face Jarrod with equanimity—might never be. That being the case she should have written more letters, even if he did not reply. Even if it meant living with Stewart as his mistress, perhaps only being able to join him in Canada when they were able to get married. For sooner or later, she thought, Jarrod would have had to give in to her demands.

'See the kudu, Stewart?' Jarrod was speaking across her.

'No . . . Yes!' There was sudden enthusiasm in her fiancé's voice. 'That's a kudu?'

'A kudu bull. Look at the white ripples striping the body. And the horns. Most distinctive.' Jarrod paused, then said, 'And there's his mate.'

'I don't see it.'

'You will,' Jarrod told him. 'She behind that clump of acacias. She'll join her man, though she may take her sweet time about it. See her, Cathy?'

A laconic statement, but purposeful all the same. Had Stewart picked up the double meaning? Probably not, for he was peering through his window, eagerly intent on catching the kudu cow when it came. Cathy doubted he had even taken in Jarrod's last words.

'Of course,' she said shortly. 'I'm used to the bush, remember?'

'It's home,' Jarrod said softly. 'It's different for Stewart.'

The breath stopped in her throat as she swung round to look at him. He was ready for her, dark eyes filled with the still unfamiliar mockery, lips lifted slightly at the corners. It's not my home any longer, she had been going to say, but once again she found herself checking the words. Jarrod was out to provoke her. He would match her words with deadlier ones of his own, spoken in that calm laconic way that was new in him.

Wiser to keep silent. Stewart was still intent on the scene beyond the window, unaware that another scene was being played out in the car. Better by far that he should remain ignorant of what was happening. Clenching her nails into the palms of her hands, she met Jarrod's look with a hard steady one of her own, then turned away from him.

The lovely sight of the kudu should produce some emotion in her, for she had been away from the bushveld for almost a year, and might never see it again. But she was far too wrought-up to enjoy herself. Jarrod was playing a game. It Stewart was unaware of it, she was not. It was a game full of hidden meanings. Gently done, and the more fiendish for it. Only a couple of hours at Marakizi, and already Cathy quivered with tension. How would she endure a whole week?

They drove on, stopping to watch a wart-hog amble comically across the road, to admire a herd of zebra, to laugh at monkeys swinging from the branches of trees while baboons made rude signs from the road.

Stewart was enchanted. He had not wanted to come to Marakizi, but now that he was here he seemed to have accepted the situation, was even looking on it as some kind of new experience. His reaction surprised Cathy. Whether he knew it or not, Stewart was giving points to Jarrod.

Points. Irritably she caught herself at the word. This was not some kind of contest. Or if it was, the outcome had already been decided. More credit to Stewart that he could rise to a situation over which he had no control. Cathy knew she could not behave with such resignation and good grace.

And then they saw the giraffe. And her pulses

quickened. Involuntarily she swung round to Jarrod. 'One of . . . yours?'

He had been waiting for her, she saw at once. And he'd caught the momentary break in her words. Had known that she had so nearly used the word 'ours'.

He nodded.

'It has a transmitter?'

So she was interested. It proved nothing.

'Yes. Like to take a peek through the binoculars?'

Oh yes, she wanted just that. 'Not particularly.' She shook her head as she said the words, keeping her hands firmly in her lap.

'Transmitter?' Stewart asked intrigued.

Jarrod said, 'Cathy may have told you that I'm doing research into the habits of giraffe. We can't follow them around the veld, of course, and so we implant tiny radio transmitters on the heads of selected animals. That way we get to learn quite a lot about them.'

'Amazing,' was Stewart's comment.

Amazing? Yes, perhaps. Interesting and exciting, too. And fun. Such fun. Fun was the main word that came to mind now. The day she and Jarrod had sedated their first giraffe just long enough to attach the radio transmitter to its head was vivid in Cathy's mind.

'Remember Daisy?' she heard Jarrod ask.

'Yes! Our first attempt.'

'You wanted to put the transmitter on her nose.'

'Big deal. You were frustrated because she wriggled at a crucial moment.' Cathy laughed at the memory, the sound clear and joyous.

'But we learned.' Jarrod's voice was low and vital, his warm breath fanned her cheek.

She turned to look at him, held the glance of the dark eyes, and felt a nerve quivering in her spine.

'We learned many things,' Jarrod said softly. 'Didn't we, Cathy?'

It was hard to breathe. Don't do this, Jarrod. Don't do this to me.

'It's very hot,' Stewart said into the silence.

'Didn't we, Cathy?' Jarrod said again.

She wouldn't give him the satisfaction of an answer. She drew a breath, wished it was steadier, and swung her head forwards.

'It's very hot in here,' Stewart said again.

'So it is,' Cathy agreed. For the first time she became aware of her fiancé's tension. She put her hand over his in a gesture that felt strangely defiant. 'Drive on please, Jarrod.'

'Sure,' he said easily, and a moment later the jeep was moving once more, and through the open windows came a breeze that brought some relief.

Jarrod had given in. But once more he had scored. Cathy knew it as definitely as she had ever known anything in her life.

The tension was thick in the car now. Cathy was filled with it. Beside her she felt Stewart's body, taut and rigid, as if he was no longer enjoying the drive. Only Jarrod's long body was relaxed. Damn Jarrod! He was the cause of the tension. Yet he himself was totally unaffected.

They drove slowly—speed was taboo in a game-park—and Cathy pointed out things of interest to Stewart. A herd of elephants at rest. A honey-bird in search of honey. The horn of an impala broken in some long-forgotten territorial dispute. She addressed herself very purposefully to Stewart, tried to make her voice eager—and wondered if he heard the effort. Jarrod would hear it. Would know the reason too. Jarrod who had always known her so well. She would not put herself in this position again, she vowed. If Stewart wanted to see the veld and its animals she would drive him. They would not go with Jarrod again.

And then Jarrod was taking the jeep off the road,

driving it easily across an area that was all rough open scrub.

'Where are we going . . .' she began, forgetting her intention to ignore him.

He didn't answer her. Didn't have to. For moments later she saw them.

Two giraffe. A female and male, tall and lovely. The female was pregnant. A pregnant giraffe nibbling leaves from a tree.

But the prickling on the back of Cathy's neck told her this was no ordinary giraffe. She could no more have prevented the question than she could have stopped herself breathing. 'Mindy?'

'Mindy,' he acknowledged, and she knew by his voice that he was smiling.

'Jarrod, I don't believe it! Our Mindy! When did this happen?'

'A while back. It was a case of love at first sight.'

Something in his tone brought her round to look at him, but there was nothing untoward in his expression. 'A baby,' she said after a long moment. 'Oh, how I wish I could be here to see it born.'

'You could be.'

'No, Jarrod, I couldn't.' Striving for calm, she injected firmness in her tone. 'I'll never come back. After this time . . .' Her tone became even firmer. 'By the time Mindy has her baby I will be in Canada.'

'Of course.' Jarrod's tone was impassive.

'What's so special about this giraffe?' Stewart asked.

Cathy turned in her seat, caught by the irritability in his tone. 'You don't understand,' she said eagerly. 'Mindy is special. She was a little more than a baby herself when Jarrod and I took her in. Her mother had been killed, and the poor little mite was so helpless, so vulnerable.'

And then, turning once more to the other side. 'Jarrod, do you remember that first day?'

'What do you think?' He was still smiling.

'Amos brought her to the camp in the jeep. She was still wobbly on her legs. And we gave her milk.'

'You hovered over her like an anxious mother hen,' Jarrod observed.

'You were rather anxious yourself, as I remember.'

'I was a bit,' he admitted.

'A bit! You should have seen him, Stewart. She was ill and there was some doubt as to whether she'd pull through that first night. Jarrod sat by her, looking after her.'

'And you made us both coffee and sandwiches when you weren't sitting with me.'

'It was quite a night.'

She fell silent, remembering. She and Jarrod sitting close together. The turning-point when they had realised that Mindy would make it. And then a sudden relieved coming together, so that they had made love right there, on the hay, yards away from the baby giraffe.

The memory brought a sudden flush to her cheeks, for it was obvious that Jarrod recalled the scene as vividly as she did. Looking away from him she gazed once more at the giraffe she had loved so much.

'I can see that you would have a fondness for the animal,' Stewart conceded.

'More than that. So much more.' Making a point of not looking at Jarrod, she said, 'Remember the story of Elsa the lioness? And Joy and George Adamson who took her in and let her live with them? That was how it was with Mindy. We looked after her, and she became a part of us. And then . . . Then the day came when we had to let her go.'

'Broke your heart,' Jarrod said.

'Oh yes, it did. Remember how we trained her to survive?'

'And how we loaded her in the truck and deposited her in the veld.'

'She looked so forlorn. So lonely.'

'You didn't see her at all, you were crying so hard,' Jarrod said quietly.

'It was like abandoning a child. She loved us, Jarrod, I know she did. I wanted so badly to keep her.'

'We had to let Mindy go.'

'I know.'

Cathy swallowed on the lump in her throat as she turned her eyes back to the window. So many emotions that she had thought no longer existed were surfacing inside her today, and she felt vulnerable and defenceless.

The giraffe were still picking at the leaves, seemingly oblivious of the humans who watched them. And then one animal, the female, turned away from her tree and looked straight at the car. Mindy. Cathy, taking in the long graceful neck, the gently swishing tail, the brown-spotted body, thought how lovely she was. Eyes, dark and dignified, she looked towards the car. Gazed. Gazed straight at Cathy.

'She knows me,' Cathy said, her voice choked. 'She does know me, doesn't she?'

'It's just a giraffe,' Stewart said, sounding a little irritated.

'She's Mindy!'

'Okay, but the fact that she's looking this way can't mean a thing.'

'I think she does know you, Cathy.' Jarrod's voice was quiet.

She turned to him, her, her eyes wet. 'Yes, she *does* know me. And you were right to persuade me to let her go. This is her life.'

'It's where she belongs,' Jarrod said, and his voice was softer now.

It was difficult to answer him. It was quiet in the car. Cathy felt as taut as a coiled spring, and beside her Stewart stirred restlessly. Jarrod had said nothing untoward. This *was* where Mindy belonged, in the veld, with her mate, with the baby soon to be born. Yet Cathy knew that Jarrod was conveying a message. One which was not difficult to understand. Though it was ridiculous in the circumstances. For Jarrod didn't want Cathy back in his life—his behaviour had made that clear.

It was time to get away from the scene, for there were undercurrents now that made their continued presence here unbearable. To her relief Jarrod seemed to have tired of it too, for he switched on the ignition and drove back over the scrub.

As if he had made his point and was satisfied, came the irrelevant thought.

CHAPTER FOUR

'Was it a mistake to come back here?'

'No, of course not,' Cathy said to Stewart, too quickly, too firmly.

'He's a difficult fellow, that husband of yours.'

'Ex-husband,' she corrected him. 'At least he will be an ex soon.'

It was twilight, and they were standing at the fence together, looking out across the bush. It was a time suspended between day and night. The sky was a vivid splash of colour, all the gold and orange of an African sunset. The bush was hushed and still. The stillness of suspense. For with the dark the buck and the zebra and the sturdy wildebeeste faced the danger of death. At night the lions and leopards would come out to hunt, and no grazing animal was safe.

It was a time of day that Cathy had always loved, but now she was too tense to enjoy it. Jarrod had unsettled her, and try as she would she could not seem to relax.

'He wants you back,' Stewart said.

'I don't think that's true.'

'I'm not so stupid that I don't pick up vibes, Cathy.'

No point in denying the vibes. They were there. The trick would be to ride them.

'We knew it might not be easy,' she said gently.

'I had no idea it would be like this.'

Neither did I, Cathy thought. Perhaps I was foolish. I should have known that Jarrod would do his best to make things difficult.

'Jarrod is playing a game,' she said slowly.

'And winning?' Stewart asked tensely.

'No! Not winning, no.' She hoped she sounded convincing.

'Would you go back to him?'

'Of course not! My God, Stewart, what a question!' She hesitated a moment before saying, 'It's not what Jarrod wants either.'

'Then what's it all about?' her fiancé asked moodily.

For a long moment Cathy was silent. Far away through the trees she caught movement. A giraffe, though not Mindy. Only a trained eye would have seen the animal in the half-light, but she did not point it out to Stewart. He would have taken the observation as a means of skirting the issue, and correctly so.

'I think,' she said, 'that I answered your question earlier. Before we went driving. Jarrod feels I made him suffer. Now he wants to see me suffer.'

'So he's vindictive.'

Jarrod had never been vindictive. He had always been too much of a man, too powerful, too strong and self-assured, too interested in issues rather than in personalities, to be vindictive. Could he have changed? And so much?

'I've never thought of him as vindictive,' she said in a low voice.

'Then how do you explain him?'

'I can't.'

'Why do you always feel you have to defend him?'

'I'm not defending him,' she said brittly.

After a long moment Stewart said, 'Cathy. Cathy, look at me.'

She turned her eyes very slowly, apprehension thick in her chest and throat.

'I have to know.' There was a kind of urgency in Stewart's tone. 'Do you still feel anything for him?'

'You know my feelings.' Hysteria was beginning to bubble inside her. 'I want a divorce.'

Very deliberately Stewart asked, '*Do* you still love him?'

The breath caught in her throat, making it impossible to answer. One can make a new life, she wanted to say. One can turn one's back on a man because it's the wise thing—the only thing—to do. But can one ever completely stop loving him? To do so would be to deny a past that was real and passionate and wonderful. Perhaps one can love less. Or perhaps one can love two men. None of which made very much sense.

'I have to know,' Stewart said.

'I want *you*,' she said, when she could talk again, and she hoped he did not register the evasion.

'Cathy . . .'

'I used to love Jarrod.' She was fighting for control. 'I don't love him anymore. But perhaps there's a part of me—a very tiny part, Stewart—that still has some feelings.'

'After the way he treated you!' he said flatly. 'God in heaven, Cathy, are you a masochist? How can you still want the man?'

'I *don't* want him! It's all over between us. You know that! I want *you*. I want to be your wife.' Her voice was trembling. 'All this . . . Marakizi and Jarrod . . . It's the past, Stewart. You are the future.'

'I want to believe you.'

'We're talking too damn much,' she said fiercely. 'Kiss me, Stewart. Kiss me, darling.'

'Cathy . . .'

'Kiss me!'

Without waiting for him to make the first move, she came to him and put her arms around his neck and drew his head down to her. His arms went around her and he kissed her quite gently. She kissed him with a fervour born of despair. This man was going to be her husband. She wanted his arms around her, wanted

him to make love to her. True, there was no wild
stirring of her blood—and how she could be stirred!—
but that was only because she was tired and confused.
With time their lovemaking would become the
beautiful thing she knew it could be.

She wasn't sure what made her look across
Stewart's shoulder. Jarrod was watching them, his
eyes sardonic. As she met his gaze he lifted an
eyebrow.

'Sorry to intrude.' His tone mocked them both.

He wasn't sorry at all. How long had he been
watching them? How much had he overheard?

Stewart had swung round at the sound of Jarrod's
voice. Cathy did not move away from him and his
arms remained around her. In challenge.

'Yes, you're intruding,' Cathy responded tersely.
'Want something?'

'To invite you for supper.'

Damn him for his infuriating calmness! Cathy and
Stewart together, a distinct case of two against one,
and yet Jarrod had the air of one who had the upper
hand.

'We don't seem to have an alternative,' Stewart said,
before Cathy could come up with an answer.

Jarrod gave a pleasant smile. Stewart's arms
tightened around Cathy, and she heard him suck in his
breath. Jarrod was getting to him, as he was getting to
her. But he was being so pleasant about it that one
could not fault him in words.

'If you have a few moments I'll show you to your
rooms.' His tone was as even and as pleasant as his
smile.

'Why now?' Stewart asked irritably.

'Because it will be dark soon.'

'Jarrod is right,' Cathy agreed wearily. 'But there's
no need to accompany us. I haven't forgotten my way
around Marakizi.'

'In that case,' Jarrod said, 'you might show Stewart to the leopard-room. You can take the cheetah.'

So crisp, so authoritative. Not as if this had once been her home also.

The guest-rooms were adjoining. There was a time when Cathy would not have believed that she would one day be a guest at Marakizi.

Leaving Stewart at the leopard-room, so called because of the ceramic tile with a picture of a leopard on the outside—she opened the door of the cheetah-room. Only to draw in her breath. On a wall hung a picture. There were other things in the room—a double bed, an oak desk and a comfortable chair, an old and lovely wardrobe. All carefully chosen. But Cathy saw none of these. She saw only the picture.

How excited they'd been when they had seen it in the gallery in Johannesburg. They had walked in on impulse, had looked at the works of the artist whose name at the time had meant nothing to them. Though they had liked his work they had no thoughts of buying. And then Cathy had seen the still-life and had fallen in love with it. Such a simple picture, flowers in a vase, but beautifully executed in a soft mixture of turquoise and blue, vase and flowers and background all blending together.

'I love it!' she had exclaimed.

'I'll buy it for you.'

She had turned shining eyes on her husband. 'Oh, Jarrod! Will you?'

'Haven't I just said so?' He had looked amused.

He had never refused her anything. She had only to voice a wish for him to grant it. Until that last time. When it had mattered. And then he had failed her.

They had hung the picture on the wall opposite their bed. It was the first thing Cathy saw when she woke in the mornings, and it never failed to delight her.

Why had Jarrod moved the picture? Why was it in the guest-room? Knowing the memories it would evoke, had he hung it here deliberately? For it did bring memories. Nights of timeless love, when it had never occurred to Cathy that what she shared with her husband would ever end. *Could* end.

As she put down her case she pushed the thought from her mind. It was time to stop thinking about Jarrod, about his reasons for doing things. The time for memories was past too. And she knew that while she was at Marakizi it would take all her strength to keep the memories at bay. Superhuman strength.

Did she have such strength?

'Why did you move the picture?' she demanded a little later.

It was dark now, and Jarrod stood by the fire, turning a piece of steak speared on the end of a long fork. The glow of the embers shed just sufficient light to reveal his shrug.

'Why?' Cathy asked again.

'Why not?' he countered laconically.

'What picture?' Stewart asked, but Cathy did not hear him.

'You know how much it meant to me.' There was a hint of passion in her tone. 'It belonged in my bedroom.'

Jarrod moved to look at her. '*Our* bedroom', he said in a tone that turned her blood first to fire then to ice.

'I know, but . . .' she began helplessly.

'My bedroom now,' he went on ruthlessly. 'You've no claims on it any more.'

Did he have to be so cruel?

'Why?' she asked again.

'It's what I wanted.' His tone crisp.

She should leave the subject alone. She was too emotional, too wrought-up, to discuss it rationally. But something stronger than reason drove her to continue. 'A guest-room, Jarrod. Just for ... for anyone ...'

'Anyone,' he agreed politely.

Feeling as hurt as if he'd dealt her a physical blow, she took a step back. Anyone. That was what she had become to Jarrod. A person with no particular meaning.

Which was as it should be, she realised a minute later. Their life together was over. She was still his wife, but in legal terms only. Soon there would be nothing left to bind them even legally. Instead there would be Stewart, and Canada, and the promise of a new life. The thought should please her. And she wondered why she felt quite so empty.

The evening braaivleis had been a kind of ritual, a special time for them both. Sitting beneath the stars, with animal and insect sounds all around them, with the evocative smell of the braaing meat in their nostrils, it had been a time for sharing, for talking. A quiet peaceful time. And yet exciting too, for always it had been a prelude to love.

Almost every night they had made love. After a marvellous honeymoon, filled with a passion that Cathy had not known existed, she had thought that marriage would be a settling-down experience, that their love-life would become less frequent, less intense. But if anything, it had become even more satisfying. Jarrod was not only a physical man in appearance. He was physical in his wants and needs. Yet tender too, with a tenderness which, at the start of their marriage, had taken Cathy by surprise. In a man as big and as powerful as Jarrod, such tenderness was almost unbearably poignant and sensuous.

But it was not only Jarrod who had desired the

nightly lovemaking. Innocent until she had met him, ignorant of her body and her emotions, Cathy had had no inkling of her own sensuousness. It was Jarrod who had awakened her. And what an awakening it had been. Rapturous, tumultuous, a mutual giving and taking that was never enough, never too much.

A gnawing that was almost like pain, began in her loins now. A familiar gnawing. And yet unfamiliar too, for in the past year she had not thought of their lovemaking. Had not allowed herself to think.

Restlessly she shifted her feet on the soft sand. A pebble caught in her open sandal, wedging itself between her toes, and she welcomed the irritation. She *would not* think about Jarrod. About their life together. It was over. Almost over. There was the divorce to be endured—'endure' was a strong word with particular connotations, why had she chosen it?—and when the final decree was granted there would be freedom. And the start of a new chapter.

Trying to ignore the gnawing that had become an ache, she wished she did not feel as if she was mourning for something that had disappeared from her life. If it was loving she needed, she would have that with Stewart. So far they had never done more than kiss. But that was not Stewart's fault. Whenever he touched her he was frustrated because she would not let him take her to bed. Always it had been Cathy who had drawn back.

But no more. There was no reason to wait till they were married. She would let him make love to her soon, though not tonight, for there was something sacrilegious in the idea of sharing his bed at Marakizi.

But soon. Across the crackling fire she sent the silent message to Stewart. Soon, Stewart dear. Soon.

The meat was ready, and they ate. Cathy had almost forgotten the special taste of steak and boerewors braaied over a coal fire. She had forgotten the succulence of hot mealies dripping with butter, the aroma of strong coffee kept heated in a jug at one end of the grid.

'I'd forgotten . . .' she said without thinking.

'Fogotten what?' Stewart sounded strained. He had been strained for much of the day.

'You didn't forget.' There was that smile again in Jarrod's voice. 'You just buried the knowledge in your subconscious.'

And she knew that even without having put the thought into words Jarrod knew what she was thinking. Again, as he had always known.

She turned suddenly, less aware of footsteps on the silent ground than of a presence. 'Amos!' The name rang out gladly.

The tall dark-skinned man stood still a moment in utter astonishment. Then his teeth shone strong and white in a broad grin of welcome. 'You're back, Miss Cathy.'

'What is it, Amos?' Jarrod's tone was oddly abrupt.

'The lion . . .'

'Right.' The word was clipped. Almost as if Jarrod was cutting Amos off. Turning briefly, Jarrod said to Cathy and Stewart, 'Excuse me,' and walked into the darkness.

'I wondered where Amos was,' Cathy mused.

'Who is he?' Stewart asked.

'Head-ranger. Jarrod's right-hand man. He's quite old, Stewart, though you'd never think it to look at him. And there's nothing, absolutely nothing, that he doesn't know about the animals and the veld.'

'Like your Jarrod?'

Cathy caught the tone as much as the use of the word 'your'. 'That's not fair,' she protested. 'He's not "my" anything, and you know it.'

'I'm sorry.' And still, Cathy thought, he was jealous.

'We only came to Marakizi to pressure Jarrod into giving me a divorce,' she said gently.

'Yes.' The note of strain was back in Stewart's voice. 'It must be this place. It's getting to me.'

'At one point this afternoon I thought you were enjoying yourself. The drive, the animals.'

'I was making the best of things. Thought I'd get a taste of the bushveld while it was available.'

'And now you regret it.'

'There are under-currents here, Cathy.'

'You're making too much of things,' she said soothingly.

But she knew what he meant.

Jarrod came back to the fire, and Cathy looked at him curiously. For Amos to call him away when he was eating was unusual. She waited for him to speak, but he merely picked up his plate of food as if nothing had happened.

'What was that all about?' she asked, when she could no longer contain her curiosity.

'Amos wanted a word with me.'

'I'm not deaf, Jarrod. And I know when something is out of the ordinary. What was that about a lion? Trouble?'

'A lion's making a nuisance of itself at the kraals.'

'People have been hurt?' she asked with swift concern, understanding the havoc a wayward lion would be able to cause amidst the thatched huts of the tribal people.

'A woman almost mauled.'

'Oh, Jarrod, that's terrible! Once it starts ... Are you going after it?'

Jarrod gave a short humourless laugh. 'Not that easy, I'm afraid. The beast's been eluding us.'

Now Cathy's interest was really caught. 'It's not the first time then?'

'No.'

'How long has this been going on?'

For the first time Jarrod hesitated. 'A while.' And then, with the urbane tone of the good host, 'Stewart, your glass is empty. Another beer?'

'Are you going after it?' Cathy was not to be thrown off.

Jarrod turned his head, his expression, what she could see of it in the dark, impassive. 'The lion?'

'Yes.' Impatiently. 'Are you going after it?'

'Of course.'

'How many times have you already been?'

Again the brief hesitation. Then Jarrod said, 'Can we talk about something else?'

A year ago she would have said, 'No! I demand to know what you intend doing. It's my right.'

But she had lost that right, and it was immaterial whether that was her fault or Jarrod's.

Be careful. The words hovered on her lips. Be careful of the lion, Jarrod. But they remained unsaid. She'd lost the right to caution him also.

They went on eating, and Jarrod's mood changed. The mere thought of a skittish lion was enough to fill Cathy with terror, and yet she responded to the change of mood. She could not help it. Just as Stewart could not help himself.

Jarrod was like a sorcerer of old, shaping their mood to his whims. Teasing, talking, laughing at them and himself. And, finally, getting them to laugh with him. There was no resisting him. He was the puppeteer, pulling the strings—as he had pulled them in other ways today—and Cathy and Stewart were born along on the tide of his buoyancy.

If Jarrod was concerned about the lion there was nothing to show it. Finally Cathy came to the conclusion that although he must be concerned, he knew what he had to do. And he did not want to discuss the matter.

An elephant roared, the bellow rolling and echoing through the darkness. Cathy sat up straight, thrilling to the sound.

'The great Lenny himself,' Jarrod grinned.

'Old Roger, surely.' Cathy spoke to Jarrod across Stewart.

'Lenny more likely,' Jarrod said.

'Old Roger's bellow, I could swear to it.'

Jarrod chuckled. 'You always had a soft spot for that rogue. No Cathy, that's Lenny all right.'

'Want to bet on it?' she asked impulsively, regretting the question the moment it was out.

'I didn't think you were the betting kind,' Stewart said. 'Why Cathy, I tried to make a bet with you that Mrs Fairchild would choose pink walls for her bedroom and you wouldn't take me on.'

'Ah, Stewart, our Cathy's a betting-lady,' Jarrod said wickedly. 'If you're going to marry her you should know that.'

'You surprise me.' Cathy could actually hear Stewart's frown. 'Cathy, you did tell me you don't put money on a bet.'

'We used a different currency.' The devil was in Jarrod tonight, no doubt about that, and Cathy shifted in her chair, wondering if she had ever really known him.

'This is childish,' she said uneasily. 'Anyway, you're probably right, Lenny it must be.'

But Stewart was determined to fall into the trap Jarrod had laid for him. 'A different currency?'

'Kisses,' Jarrod said. And into the silence that fell after the word, 'A most satifying form of currency.'

'Jarrod!' Cathy protested, after a look at Stewart's stunned expression.

'With money,' Jarrod went on undaunted, 'one person has to lose. With kisses both parties end up winning.'

'That was unnecessary,' Cathy bit out tersely,

feeling Stewart's body go rigid beside her.

'Do you think so? I thought it was a piece of advice Stewart might like to take into married life with him. A wedding present from me you might say.'

'I don't need advice of that sort,' Stewart said very correctly, and Cathy put in,

'Don't you know when you've overstepped the limits of decency?'

'Limits of decency,' Jarrod mocked. 'My God, Cathy, has all this time away from me turned you stuffy? Just as well in the circumstances that our marriage is ending. I never could stand a stuffy woman.'

That hurt, as it had been meant to. Cathy sat straight and stiff in her deck-chair, staring unhappily into the fire. So Jarrod was glad the marriage was over. He would put no obstacles in their path. And she knew it was silly that she should feel quite so shattered at the idea that he wanted finality as much as she did.

Jarrod laughed suddenly. The sound was low and vital in the darkness. Infinitely seductive. Cathy's nerves tingled, and the ache of longing she'd felt earlier started again. So appalled was she at the depths of her desire, that in reaction she moved a few inches closer to Stewart. It was obscene that she should feel a real sense of loss at the knowledge that she would never lie in Jarrod's arms again.

Physical attraction had always been strong between Jarrod and herself. Her husband had never had to exert himself to excite her. Mere proximity to the rugged face and powerful body had been sufficient to arouse desire in her. Sex was the one thing that had never been a problem in their life together.

But sex was only one facet of married life, she reminded herself, not for the first time today. There were other factors that counted as much—no, *more*—if a marriage was to be happy.

A woman needed security. She had to know that she could depend on her husband. She had loved Jarrod. Oh, how she had loved him! But when the crisis had come he had not been there for her. When she had needed him most he had put his own interests first. For that she would never forgive him.

'You seem determined to make things as difficult as possible, Jarrod,' Stewart said grimly.

'On the contrary.' The amusement had left Jarrod's voice. 'I think I'm being extremely reasonable. You barge in here with my wife. You ask—no, you demand—that I release her so that you can have her instead. And then you say I make things difficult!'

'You don't want her,' Stewart said.

'Did I say that?'

There was nothing in his tone to give Cathy joy. Instead she was reminded of two dogs, bristling and angry in their squabble over the same bone. She felt irritated.

'Your actions say it all for you,' she accused.

Stewart said, 'We can't stay here a week.'

'You know my terms.' Jarrod spoke quite pleasantly.

'It's really impossible.' This from Stewart.

'It doesn't have to be. Why not look at it as a holiday in the bushveld before you hit the icy wastes of Canada? Relax, you might just enjoy yourselves.'

'Not likely.' Stewart sounded more grim than before, and Cathy wondered how long it would take for the two men to go at each other physically. A holiday it would not be if Jarrod persisted with his taunts. She was relieved when Stewart got to his feet and said he was going to bed.

Leaving Jarrod with the embers of the dying fire, they walked together to the adjoining guest-rooms.

'Stay with me tonight,' Stewart pleaded at the door of the leopard-room.

'I can't.'

'Please.' He drew her into the circle of his arms. 'It would go a long way to making the week bearable.'

'I can't. Stewart, don't press me.'

He looked down at her, and in the dim light of the moon she saw the set of his jaw. 'Will things ever be any different? I won't put up with a sexless relationship.'

'It won't be,' Cathy promised. 'But not here, Stewart. I can't. I just can't . . .'

'I think you're scared of Jarrod.'

'That's ridiculous, it has nothing to do with him,' she countered too swiftly. And then, on a steadier note, 'We have a lifetime before us, darling. Let's not start our loving at Marakizi.'

Stewart's arms dropped to his side. 'Perhaps you're right,' he agreed moodily. 'Marakizi means Jarrod, and I don't want any reminders of that man each time we're in bed together.'

'There won't be,' she said gratefully, wishing that Jarrod had a fraction of Stewart's sensitivity.

'I want no ghosts in our marriage, Cathy.'

'No ghosts,' she promised him. She put her arms around his neck and kissed him. 'Sleep well, Stewart my love.'

CHAPTER FIVE

TWENTY minutes in the cheetah-room, with the picture opposite the bed, were enough to convince Cathy that there would be no sleep for her. Closing the door softly, so that Stewart would not hear the sound, she went outside.

The compound was dark, with only the light of the stars and the slender moon to show the way. What was left of the camp-fire had been extinguished. The camp-staff had retired early, and even Jarrod must be on his way to bed. Cathy glanced in the direction of their bungalow—*his* bungalow—but the window faced the other way so that she could not see if a light still shone there.

A hyena's laugh rent the stillness, but Cathy's steps did not falter. The dark bushveld and the animals that might lurk in the long dry grass beyond the fence of the compound held no dangers for her. The only danger came from Jarrod, from feelings and sensations which would not be suppressed no matter how hard Cathy tried.

Almost of their own accord Cathy's feet trod the familiar path that paralleled the fence, stopping at the spot where her elbows had worn two indentations in the wood from the many times when she had stood here in the past. The indentations were unchanged, and her elbows slipped into them easily.

What could have possessed her to come back to Marakizi? She wondered as she stared into the darkness. She should have known Jarrod well enough to understand that he would be difficult. The Jarrod she had loved and lived with had not been difficult, the mockery she had seen in him all day was new to him—but all the same she should have known. She should have waited until he desired a divorce as much as she did.

'It was a mistake to come here.'

'Was it?'

She had not realised she had spoken the words out loud. On an indrawn breath she spun round to find Jarrod beside her.

'Yes! What are you doing here, Jarrod?'

'Waiting for you.'

'We had no arrangement.'

'We didn't need one.' Softly he added, 'We were always able to communicate without words, Cathy.'

A rush of feeling overwhelmed her, an intensification of the ache and the hunger and the longing that she'd been trying to ignore. Her legs were weak and for a moment she found herself swaying towards him. And then she remembered Stewart. Stewart who lay unsuspecting in the leopard-room. Stewart who was going to be her husband.

Her voice was deliberately harsh as she said, 'We need words now. Dredging up the betting-kisses was a low trick. Why did you do it?'

Jarrod laughed. 'Just teasing.'

'That's your idea of teasing?' She tossed the words at him through the rush of blood in her head.

'Come on, Cathy, you used to have a sense of humour.'

A breeze stirred the bush, mingling with the warmth of Jarrod's breath to touch her cheek. Cathy had not realised quite how close he was to her. Suddenly she was trembling. 'Coming back here must have made it desert me.'

'So it seems. Our kissing-bets were always special to us, Cathy.'

'That's so,' she acknowledged reluctantly, taking a step away from him. 'But that was when . . .'

'When,' he prompted.

'When we loved each other.' After a moment, when Jarrod did not speak, Cathy said, 'You know yourself that everything is different now.'

'It is, isn't it?' he agreed reflectively.

Part of her had hoped, quite irrationally, for a denial. Defensively she said, 'You know it is. You've been baiting Stewart all day. The kissing-bet was the last straw. Jarrod, why?'

'I've already told you I was teasing.'

'You were provoking Stewart. And embarrassing me.'

'I wouldn't have thought either of you would be embarrassed.'

'Then you're insensitive.'

'Or perhaps there isn't the ease between the two of you that there should be.'

'Now you're being insulting.'

A hand touched her arm, the thumb brushing upwards and inwards to the sensitive area of her inner arm. 'Why aren't you in Stewart's room?'

She strove for control. 'Not for want of an invitation on his part or willingness on mine. But I told you earlier, we won't be sharing a room while we're at Marakizi.'

'Noble,' he said drily. 'That needn't have stopped you from getting together for some clandestine lovemaking.'

She had been thinking along the same lines. 'It's really none of your business,' she said loftily, and wondered why she had not stayed with Stewart. She could have gone to her own room after a while.

'Strictly speaking it isn't,' Jarrod agreed. 'But I can't help being interested in the fact that my wife has changed so much.'

'I'm not interested in discussing it.'

'I am,' he drawled insolently. 'The wife I remember was sensual and passionate. All fire when she was roused. No proprieties would have stopped her from making love when she felt like it. Perhaps she'd have slipped back to her own room later for decency's sake, but she'd have made love first.'

He was so to the point that there was nothing she could say. Before she'd met Jarrod, Cathy had not suspected the depths of her passion, but Jarrod had woken her, had taught her. She and Jarrod had been drawn together like magnets. And the pull between them had never waned.

She gripped the fence tightly, pretending to see something in the darkness, wishing that Jarrod would just disappear. Knowing he would not.

'Why Stewart?' he asked at length.

'He's the right man for me.'

'Do you love him?'

'Of course,' she said jerkily.

'With your mind maybe.'

She refused to look at him, 'Now what's that supposed to mean?'

'The chemistry is all wrong.'

'Because I'm not in his bed at this moment?'

'That's one reason.'

'I've matured, Jarrod.'

'Do you call suppressing your passions mature? Or are you lying to yourself?'

'Stop baiting me!'

'I saw the kiss by the fence, remember?' He touched her arm again, fingers sliding along her skin with a sensuousness that was well-nigh unbearable. 'I detected your lack of enthusiasm.'

'Not true,' she defended. 'I was enjoying every moment.'

'You were pretending. You were making a grand effort, but the wamth and the passion were lacking.'

Again she was silent. Jarrod knew her so well. Tensely she stared into the dark veld.

'You never had to make an effort with me, Cathy. Fire and fire, that's what we were. Always.'

'So we were. And look where it led us!' She turned to him, distraught. 'You're trying to tell me our chemistry was right. All right then, it was. But you failed me when I needed you. You didn't love me enough. The sex was there, Jarrod, but not the love.'

His fingers tightened cruelly on her arm. 'You have all the answers.'

'Not all, but I do have some. You're getting through to me, Jarrod. Why Stewart, that's what you want to know. Well, I'll tell you. There's more to marriage than sex, I learned that to my cost. There's dependability and kindness and stability. And a husband who's within reach when you need him.'

'You were never the kind of woman who wanted a man with a nine-to-five job and a house and car in the suburbs.'

'I am now,' she flashed at him.

'You've changed so much, Cathy?'

'Yes, damn you, I have, and all your scorn is not going to make me say otherwise. We were playing at marriage, Jarrod. Marakizi and the research, it all seemed so wonderful at first.'

'It doesn't any longer?'

'That house in suburbia has extraordinary appeal for me now. It's what I *want*, Jarrod. And I want Stewart.'

'And you'll never miss what we had?'

'Stop this, Jarrod!'

'Well, will you?' His voice was harsh. 'Be honest, Cathy.'

'You can't do this to me.' Her throat was thick, and her eyes were heavy with tears.

'The hell I can't! When Stewart makes love to you,

and you give him your dutiful little responses, will there be memories?' Jarrod was relentless.

'I won't listen to this!' She tried to move away from him, but his other hand caught her waist, imprisoning her.

'I think you'll remember what love is really like. The hunger and the fire and the marvel of release.'

She trembled. 'Why are you doing this to me?'

'To shake you out of your complacency.'

'No, Jarrod, that's not it. You don't want me in your life, you've made that plain enough. Yet you can't bear to see me happy with someone else. You said earlier today that you'd suffered. And so now you're making me suffer.'

'What a long speech,' Jarrod said coldly, but she felt hot anger in his hands, and she was excited by it. He laughed suddenly, the sound vital in the stillness. 'I really did touch you on the raw when I reminded you that you're a passionate woman. In that respect, at least, I don't believe you've changed. So there will be memories.'

'You've made sure of the memories,' she said bitterly. 'Starting with Jock, the memories have tormented me all day. Oh, I don't blame you for Jock, that gorgeous hound is a part of Marakizi, and I'd have wondered where he was if he hadn't come rushing to greet me. But everything else . . . My lovely picture. I couldn't understand why you'd taken it out of our—your bedroom and hung it in the cheetah-room, but now I do. And Mindy. You knew just where to find her, and you didn't have to guess very hard to know I'd be emotional when I saw her. And then at the fire, talkng about the elephants, that was just more of the same.'

'You have it all worked out, don't you?'

'You bet I have. Down to knowing why you're doing it. It's part of your plan to make me suffer.

You're enjoying that, aren't you, Jarrod? Just as you're enjoying making poor Stewart squirm"

'It's his choice if he squirms,' Jarrod said levelly.

'This is your territory, and you're so much the master of it. Perhaps you'd feel differently if you were in the city, if you were in Stewart's office. That's his territory, Jarrod. It's where he designs his buildings.'

'And where you design pink-walled bedrooms for rich women.'

'Wrong. I don't work for Stewart. My job is with a decorating firm.'

'With a boss who turned you from an unaffected girl of the veld into a sophisticated city lady.'

She felt herself flush in the darkness. 'I knew we'd get to my appearance sooner or later. I take it you don't like the way I look.'

'Very chic, but somewhat different from the barefoot windswept Cathy I remember.'

The words were evocative, bringing back more memories. Cathy and Jarrod travelling in an open truck, Cathy's hair blown by the wind, tossed backward as she laughed at something Jarrod said, and Jarrod drawing the hair across his mouth before kissing her. Cathy and Jarrod late at night in their room, bare feet sharing the same footstool as they drank hot coffee and reviewed the day's work.

So many memories. Some warm, some amusing, others sensual. All of them poignant.

She made to move away from him, but his hand tightened on her. 'Does Stewart know the old Cathy?'

'Jarrod . . .'

'The girl who wore her hair loose, and lived in shorts and sandals when she wore shoes at all? Does he know the Cathy who needed no make-up because her eyes sparkled and her lips and cheeks were rosy from the sun?'

Briefly she closed her eyes. Then she said, 'I know what you're trying to do. I was one woman for you,

Jarrod, I'm another for Stewart. My life has changed, and I've had to change with it. And no amount of taunting on your part will make me feel guilty about it.'

'And you're happy?'

'Yes, damn you,' she said fiercely. 'I'm very happy indeed.'

'I'm glad,' he said, and she knew he was lying. 'Do you ever miss your sketching?'

'I've turned my art in a different direction,' she responded flatly. 'I can't take any more of this, Jarrod. Let me go. I'm going to my room.'

Still he held her. 'In a moment.'

'I can't take it! I've had enough.'

His hands dropped then, and his voice was softer. 'Stay, Cathy. We haven't talked.'

'We've talked too much.'

'No, Cathy.'

The strange gentle voice kept her where she was. But she did not trust him. 'We've nothing to talk about. Except the divorce. Give me the consent, Jarrod, that's all I ask of you.'

'In good time, I've told you that.'

'I really do want to go inside.'

'Liar,' he said cheerfully. 'Tell me how you find Marakizi.'

She looked at him uncertainly. 'Now?'

'It's as good a time as any, no Stewart around.' He touched her cheek flatteringly. 'Don't bristle at that, I just mean it's easier for us to talk alone.'

'I don't think Stewart would approve.'

'Don't tell him then. I'm really interested.' He chuckled softly. 'Perhaps I have been a tease, but don't see me only as an ogre. You've been away a long time, Cathy.'

She took a few steps away from him, and felt her breathing ease. With some distance between herself and Jarrod she felt safer.

'I've missed Marakizi,' she said at length.

'I know.'

She leaned forward, putting her arms on the fence. For a few minutes they stood in silence, listening to the sounds of the night, the singing of the crickets, the small scufflings in the bush. 'I'd forgotten how the wood at this point was shaped to my arms,' she said.

Jarrod gave a soft laugh. 'Your favourite spot in the compound. It wasn't hard to know where to find you.'

'Where's Jock?'

'Indoors. And raging at his impotence. I've kept him inside at night since the tussle with the baboon.'

'Poor Jock.' Cathy laughed too, for the first time. 'His pride was hurt more than his hide, I think.'

'I think you're right.'

They were silent again, and then Cathy said, 'In time Stewart and I will have memories too.'

'I'm sure you will.'

It was an easy response. It was absurd that Cathy should wish Jarrod more perturbed.

A little tartly she asked, 'What about you, Jarrod? Have there been any women in your life recently?'

'Why the question?' No change in the easy tenor of his voice.

'Helen is one of them, I'll bet.'

'Stop fishing, Cathy. You have a man, I'm entitled to some fun of my own.'

If only he knew how little fun she'd had since she'd left him. The men she had dated had been few and far between. Apart from Stewart she had seen no man more than once, for each one had only had bed in mind, and that was not how she had wanted the evenings to end. One-night stands were not her scene. Besides, Jarrod had spoiled her, so that the thought of making love with another man had been distasteful. And then Stewart had come along. Although she had not yet allowed him to make love to her, she sensed that with undemanding, gentle Stewart she would be able to let herself love again.

She wished that the thought of Jarrod with other women didn't hurt quite so much. She knew her jealousy was unreasonable, but reason had little to do with her feelings.

'You were never a man who liked the solo life,' she observed.

'How well you know me.' His voice was softly seductive. Feeling uncomfortably out of her depth, Cathy was sorry she had raised the topic. She was relieved when Jarrod said, 'We were talking about Marakizi.'

For a while they discussed Jarrod's work. Cathy was deeply interested to hear how the research was developing. There had been progress, though less than she would have expected. 'Things take time,' Jarrod said at her comment.

The research had been a project that had involved them both. The scientific areas had been Jarrod's. The illustrations—for every aspect of giraffe life had been photographed and sketched—had been Cathy's. But in all things their interests had overlapped, each had been enthusiastic about the work the other was doing. As she listened to Jarrod talk, Cathy grieved that she would not be in on the final stages of the research and on the compiling of the book that would flow quite naturally there from. Helen would help Jarrod, she guessed. She was no mean hand with a sketching pencil, and Jarrod would be happy to give her a camera and equipment.

Cathy tried to push away her feelings of depression. Let Helen pick up where she herself had left off, she tried to tell herself. She should be glad that the project had not come to an end when she had left Marakizi. Whatever Jarrod's faults might be, he was a dedicated scientist and the work he was doing would be of value to generations of zoologists. If Helen stepped into the gap left in Jarrod's personal life—well, even that must be accepted. Cathy had Stewart and a new career, soon she would have a new home. It would be crazy even to think that Jarrod's own life could remain unchanged.

Quietly she listened to him, interjecting a question here and there, content for the most part to hear him talk. She had forgotten quite how low and vital his voice was, how much the sound of it pleased her. She had forgotten the enthusiasm he put into his work, and the vividness that went into the telling of it. She had forgotten quite how much it had all meant to her.

Or had she forgotten? Perhaps she had merely pushed aside the memories, refusing to let herself think of the things that brought her pain because they were no longer with her. But forgotten? Oh no, she knew now that she had forgotten nothing.

The return to Marakizi had brought with it emotions and sensations she had kept buried. Feelings which had once been so precious to her. There was a part of her that wanted to let those feelings surface. Another part that knew the danger of doing so.

Nostalgia was a dangerous thing, she decided. It allowed a person to dwell on the good that had happened in the past while at the same time ignoring the bad. Dwell on at your peril, she told herself grimly.

No matter that at this moment Canada seemed a distant alien place. That Stewart was almost a stranger. That he failed to stir in her the passions she knew only too well were dormant inside her. Canada would be home. Certainly it spelled security. Security was the thing she needed above all else, and only Stewart could give it to her.

Jarrod and Marakizi—a powerful combination—had cast their spell over her, making her feel restless and uncertain, filling her with a longing that was so intense that it was like a bodily ache. But dawn would bring returning sanity. She would shed the nostalgia and the longing, and she would look forward to the future with a new confidence and enthusiasm.

'I think I really will go inside,' she said when Jarrod fell silent.

'You said you'd stay a while.'

'You said it. I . . . I'm cold.'

'I'll keep you warm.' His arm went around her shoulders, and though it was their only point of contact, she was aware of every muscle and bone and sinew in the long hard body. 'I've always kept you warm in the past,' he said.

It was playing with fire to remain here when every nerve and fibre was responding to Jarrod, when her nostrils were filled with the smell of him, when she ached to make love with him—and yet something stronger than her own self-will kept her in the shelter of his arm.

'You feel good.' He nuzzled his mouth in her hair.

'How are the lodges doing?' she asked, a little wildly.

'Very well. You smell good too.' His lips touched her ear, sending ripples of fire all the way to her throat. 'New perfume?'

'Tell me about the lodges . . .'

His lips were still in her hair. "Do you use this stuff to seduce Stewart? Does he need that kind of seduction? Your sexy body was always sufficient seduction for me.'

She tried to suppress a shudder, and knew that Jarrod was not fooled. 'I only stayed out here because you wanted to talk,' she got out, with all the severity she could summon. 'If you're not going to talk I may as well go inside.'

'The new Cathy, I keep forgetting.' She felt the

laughter in his throat. 'Let's talk then, if that's what you really want.'

It was not what she wanted, and he knew it. She wanted him to kiss her in all the ways that he knew best, and she wanted to kiss him, and she wanted to feel that strong body against hers, melting into hers.

With superhuman effort, she asked again, 'I asked how the lodges are doing.'

His lips left her hair as he lifted his head, and his arm dropped from her shoulder. Now she really did feel cold, but her pride would not allow her to go back to the warmth of his body. 'The lodges are doing well,' Jarrod said. 'Both are booked to capacity most of the time.'

She turned away from him, and leaned once more on the fence. 'Marakizi is doing well too, I can see that.'

'Right.'

'There are changes, of course. The helicopter and the 'phone.'

'I wondered when you'd get round to mentioning them again.'

She swung round to look at him. 'Did you, Jarrod? Once they would have meant everything to me.'

'Cathy . . .'

'I begged you for a 'phone. But you were so hung up on the wonders of living in the rough, that you wouldn't hear of it. No kitschy civilised touches for you, wasn't that it, Jarrod?'

'Something like it.' His voice was without expression.

'What made you decide differently?'

'The time seemed right.'

'It was never right while I was here. That's what I mean about generosity and dependability. Stewart wouldn't expect me to exist without the necessities of modern life.'

'If a 'phone and a helicopter are important to your happiness, they're here now.'

Was this Jarrod's way of asking her to come back to him? If so, it was the closest he had come to it.

'It's too late,' she said with sudden urgency. 'If the 'phone had been here when I needed it, I wouldn't have lost my baby. If you'd been here it wouldn't have happened either.'

'People make mistakes, Cathy.' Later she would remember the words and understand that they had been meant as an apology. But at this moment the hurt that had torn her apart for so long did not allow for concessions.

In a hard voice she said, 'Then don't make the same mistakes with Helen when you marry her.'

'You enjoy making assumptions,' he said coldly.

'You're far too physical a man to continue living alone.'

'Perhaps.' His voice gave nothing away.

She took a breath, willing herself to regain her composure. 'You asked me if there were changes at Marakizi. Things don't stand still in a year. The 'phone and the helicopter, they're the obvious ones. But I see other things too. New shrubs outside the lab. Less of a spring in Jock's step—I suppose he's beginning to get old, my poor dear old Jock of the Bushveld.'

'Little things,' Jarrod said.

'Little enough. You've changed too, Jarrod.'

For the first time she tried to put into words an impression that had been with her all day. 'There are lines around your eyes that I don't remember. A kind of weariness in your face.' She bit her lip, then gave voice to the question she had been wanting to ask him since the moment she'd seen him striding through the compound earlier that day. She hadn't asked it then, because the very nature of her mission was innately

hostile. And yet they were not enemies, she and Jarrod.
They were merely two people who could no longer live
together. And she had once cared for him so very much.

'Are you well, Jarrod?'

After a moment he said, 'I'm fine.'

'Jarrod?' She peered at him through the darkness,
trying to read his face, finding that difficult because in
the dim light she was unable to see his eyes.

'I'm fine,' he said again, and there was a new note in
his voice, impatience she thought.

'That's good then. I wondered.'

Silence fell. Jarrod made no effort to speak, and
Cathy did not speak either. She could have left him,
she supposed. Could have gone back to her room. But
something still kept her here. A slight breeze had
risen, and she could hear the rustling sound of the
bushes, a whispering that mingled with all the other
sounds of the night. The breeze must have blown from
the direction of the now-dead camp-fire, for just the
faintest smell of the braai still lingered on the air.

The sound and the smell of the bushveld. A special
atmosphere. She would miss it when she was in
Canada. All at once a week at Marakizi did not seem
long at all. Marakizi was part of her very soul, just as
her love for Jarrod had once been. She would savour
every sight, every sound, every smell of the place, she
decided. Would make the most of every moment. The
uneasy exchanges with Jarrod notwithstanding, she
was glad that she was out here, and not in the hot
confines of the cheetah-room.

The continuing silence was unstrained. Cathy was
busy with her thoughts, endeavouring to pick up every
impression and imprint it on her senses. Beside her, as
still as she was, Jarrod was a long taut figure. He had
lit a cigarette and the end of it glowed in the dark.

'And then there are things that haven't changed at
all,' Cathy said at last, softly.

'Such as,' he prompted.

'The veld. The atmosphere. That particular smell that will always make me think of Marakizi whenever a hint of it touches my nostrils.' She let her hands run along the worn indentation on the fence, planed to smoothness from the many times she had leaned her arms on it. 'The animals. They never change, do they Jarrod?'

'You used to enjoy the time after sunset.'

'I love it still. The cool air after the heat of the day. The utter peacefulness.'

'There's something else that hasn't changed,' Jarrod said.

The utter lack of inflexion in his tone should have warned her. But it didn't. She looked at him when he didn't elaborate, and saw that he was grinding out his cigarette beneath the sole of one shoe.

And then he reached for her, and it was too late to escape him.

CHAPTER SIX

As his lips came down on hers with an echoing of the hunger that had gnawed at her all evening, her body became one mass of sensation. Later she would wonder whether she could have resisted him. There was in fact a rational moment when she remembered Stewart, but when she got out his name Jarrod quietened her with a fierce, 'Damn Stewart, he's not with us now.'

Jarrod . . .'

'*This* hasn't changed,' he said, his voice insistent, his mouth so close to hers that he seemed to be breathing the words directly into her throat. 'The chemistry's as strong as ever, Cathy.'

'But Stewart . . .'

'Forget Stewart! I want you, Cathy. And you want me, dearest. We've been wanting each other all day.'

She could not quarrel with the statement. For as his mouth closed over hers again she knew just how badly she had been wanting him.

His kiss was a sensuous onslaught that made desire run like fire in her loins. All rational thought deserting her, she opened her mouth willingly to his, moaning in pleasure at an exploration that was mutually hungry and desperate. There was nothing tender in the kiss. They had been waiting too long for this moment to be tender. There was just heat and passion, and a thirst that seemed as if it would never be slaked.

At length they had to draw apart for breath. Cathy was seized by a violent trembling. Her legs were weak, her body burning, her heart was beating so hard that she thought it would burst from her chest.

'This hasn't changed,' Jarrod insisted again.

'No,' she agreed on a choked throat.

'Oh God, Cathy, why do you have to be so beautiful! So utterly desirable.'

This time when he kissed her there was a difference. This was a teasing of lips, a tantalising of tongue and teeth, a seduction of the senses. Jarrod cupped the small chin in a big hand, and ran his lips along her throat. How well he knew the most erotic areas, and how expertly he knew how to arouse her. As his mouth moved against her, Cathy made small animal noises of pleasure and pain, and her hands buried themselves convulsively in his hair, drawing him closer to her, wanting to melt into him.

'It's been so long,' he groaned at last. 'Too long, my dearest.'

'Too long,' she echoed him, and never knew whether she said the words aloud or not.

One hand pushed the shirt from her trousers, and caressed the smooth bare skin of her stomach, lingering there a moment before moving upwards. With an expertise born of long practice, Jarrod found the clasp of the lacy bra, and opened it, then brought his hand forward to cup the soft fullness of a breast. His fingers found the nipple and played with it till it hardened to his touch, then went to the other breast to caress that nipple likewise. And Cathy, arching towards him, thought she would faint from the pleasure of his touch.

She was all sensation now. Not a sane thought remained. There was just the heady sweetness, the seductive arousal. There was only Jarrod, caressing her, making love to her as no man had ever done before him, as no man would ever do again. There was only a passion that was primitive and primeval. As their bodies swayed together, his thighs hard and erotic in their pressure against hers, nothing mattered but the need to be one with him.

'Cathy, Cathy dearest . . . I want you.'

'Yes!'

She wanted him too. But not here, on the ground, where the earth was rough and stony.

Arms around each other they began to walk, her shoulder fitting snugly into his arm-pit, their legs and hips brushing against each other. So often had they walked this way to their bungalow, joyfully anticipating a night of love. It was all so agonisingly familiar.

They came out of the darkness that enveloped the fence to the centre of the compound where the bungalows were. Arms still tightly around each other they emerged from the trees. And then Cathy stopped in mid-step.

A light shone in Stewart's window. She could not remember whether it had been on when she'd left her room and come this way.

'My God,' she breathed, appalled.

Above her head there was an angry hiss of breath, and then the arm around her waist urged her on. But for the first time she resisted.

'Jarrod, no.'

'Come along, Cathy.' His arm moved upwards, his hand caressed her shoulder.

'We can't, don't you see?' She twisted her head to look up at him, her eyes filled with despair.

'You've got to be kidding,' he said tightly. 'You know we're going to make love.'

'No.'

'Damn you, Cathy, we're both aroused, it's what we both want.'

'We can't.' Her throat was thick with frustration and unhappiness.

'You can't pull back now. Dammit, you're not a frightened virgin. You're my wife, and we've gone too far to stop.'

'I'm Stewart's fiancée. There was more light now that they were in the main area of the compound, and she could see Jarrod's face. His jaw was an inflexible line, his skin was drawn tightly across high cheekbones. He looked as taut and as frustrated as she felt.

'Damn Stewart! You should have thought of him earlier.'

'I didn't know . . .'

'What didn't you know, my sweet wife?' His voice lashed her as his fingers, no longer seductive or gentle, bit cruelly into her soft skin. 'You played along with me. You knew how things would end the moment you found me waiting for you tonight.'

'No,' she insisted, pleaded.

'Yes.' He was relentless. 'Perhaps you comfort yourself by thinking otherwise. Oh, we made conversation, sure enough, but all the time we both knew we'd end up making love.'

'Not love. Sex.' The rapier-thrust of his voice drove her to taunt him in response. 'Sex, Jarrod, that's all it would have been. That's all it's ever been between us.'

'You little bitch,' he hissed.

'If I'm a bitch then you're a bastard. You knew exactly what you were doing. Exciting me, rousing me—yes, I was aroused, I can't deny it—when all the time Stewart was just yards away in his room.'

'You don't owe him a thing.' His voice was tight and controlled, but she sensed the fury bubbling beneath the surface of his composure.

'I owe him loyalty. Not that you'd understand a thing about it. Stewart trusted me.'

'Foolishly,' he taunted.

'Hurt me all you like, Jarrod, it won't make any difference. The answer's still no, I won't go to bed with you.' She paused to take a jagged breath. More steadily she went on. 'You'll never hurt me again as much as you hurt me all those months ago. So hurt away all you wish, it won't force me into your bed.'

'I've no intention of forcing you,' he grated, his voice icy with contempt. 'You'll come to my bed before this week is over. You'll come begging to me, because whatever else may have changed, you still want me.'

'Don't bet on it.'

'I don't need to. Go to your lonely room, Cathy. That's what you say you want. I know you won't go to your fiancé's room. Even you can't pretend that he can give you what you want from me.'

It was the one thing she really could not pretend, Cathy knew as she stared starkly at the ceiling long after Jarrod had gone to his bungalow, a taut angry figure, whistling tunelessly as he went. Stewart was a dear, but he might never be able to rouse her as Jarrod could. True, till now she had not given him the chance, yet she faced the fact all the same.

Just as she faced the fact, the painful and utterly humiliating fact, that the physical attraction between Jarrod and herself had not waned. If anything, absence had made it grow stronger, as if each had yearned for the other in the time they'd been apart.

With a little cry of despair she flung herself on to her stomach and buried her face in her pillow. For if tonight had shown that the pull between Jarrod and herself was like the force that drew magnets together, it had shown something else also. Physical attraction was all it was. There was no love, no tenderness, no gentle emotion of any kind. Had Jarrod loved her, he could have said so. The opportunity had been there. But he had not done so. What he had chosen to do, quite deliberately, was to prove a point, to show her that on a physical level she was his woman.

And he had succeeded, as he had known he would.

But sex wasn't enough. Exciting as their lovemaking could be, it was not enough. Could never be enough, as she'd learned when the crisis had occurred. There had to be loving and caring and responsibility.

Yet the pull of sexual attraction was powerful. Cathy's presence at Marakizi must be as agonising for Jarrod as it was for her. For the old feelings were still there. He wanted her, that had been no act. He wanted her in his arms, in his bed, and he was frustrated because he could not have her. Right now he must be lying awake too, as tense and as unfulfilled as she was. If he was exposing her to pain, he was putting himself at risk also. It was stupid, unreasonable. But when men were thwarted they were often unreasonable. Perhaps it did not matter to Jarrod that he would suffer, because he knew she would be suffering likewise. And that gave him satisfaction. There could be no other answer.

Dear God, let this week pass quickly, she prayed. And keep Jarrod out of my way, because I don't know how much more I can take of this.

Long before she was ready to get up, the sun slanted through the curtained window. Cathy's head ached and her eyes burned, and she wanted nothing so much as to pull the blanket over her head and catch up on the sleep she had missed. But to do so would be to excite unwelcome attention. Jarrod, guessing what kind of night she must have had, would be satisfied. Stewart would be concerned.

Dragging herself out of bed, Cathy went across to the mirror. She looked the way she felt, pale-cheeked and hollow-eyed. Beneath the tired eyes were dark smudges, and her lips were bruised. One word was sufficient to describe her appearance—terrible.

A shower revived her spirits somewhat. When she had washed her hair and towelled herself dry, she put on jeans and the crispest shirt she had brought with her. Normally she wore little make-up, but today she needed all the artifice at her disposal to repair the ravages left by Jarrod's lovemaking and the sleepless night.

She had just finished doing her face when there was a knock at the door. She was not ready to see either of her men, but of the two Stewart posed less of a threat.

'Good morning,' she smiled.

'Doesn't look that good.' Stewart did not smile back as he studied her.

Cathy felt herself stiffen, but she said, 'Oh, it's a fine morning.'

'Did you sleep well?'

Her appearance spoke for her. 'Not that well.'

'I didn't sleep well either,' he said moodily.

She looked at him remorsefully. 'Oh Stewart, I'm sorry. It's Marakizi and Jarrod, I know that.'

'Partly.' His eyes had an odd expression. 'I came to your room last night.'

A pulse beat in her throat. 'I thought I told you we couldn't . . .'

'You did, and I came nevertheless.' His voice was cold. 'You weren't there.'

Mutely she looked at him, not knowing what to say.

'You were with Jarrod, weren't you?'

She could feel hysteria bubbling inside her. 'I couldn't sleep. It was so hot and . . .' She took a breath, felt her composure returning. 'You say Marakizi is getting to you. Can you imagine what it's doing to me? I had to go outside. Please understand.'

'You haven't answered my question.'

Last night there had been Jarrod with his demands and his mockery. Now there was Stewart, and more disapproval. She wanted nothing more than to vanish from Marakizi, alone, to go some place where she would be accountable to nobody but herself.

'As it happens I did run into Jarrod.' Levelly she

looked at Stewart. And then she saw the unhappiness in his eyes, and she knew she could not be angry with him. If anything he had her sympathy. It was difficult for him to be here, he was at a natural disadvantage on another man's territory. Especially when the man was Jarrod. For his fiancé to be with that man secretly was more than Stewart should have to put up with.

'It wasn't planned.' She moved towards him, her hand making a little gesture of apology and appeal.

Stewart's expression remained unyielding. After a moment her hand dropped to her side.

Unsteadily Cathy said, 'The compound is so small. It's difficult to avoid Jarrod, but I didn't plan to meet him.' And on a harder note. 'My God, Stewart, you might believe me. Do you think I'd have gone out in the dark if I'd known I'd see him?'

Tensely she watched him, waiting for the next question. She could hear the words even before he uttered them. Did you make love?

How to answer? Her lips and tongue could form the lie easily enough, but her eyes would give her away.

Either Stewart trusted her, or he knew the answer already and did not want to hear it spoken aloud. Whatever the case, he did not voice the question. Instead, jaw set, expression grim, he only asked grimly, 'Is this how it's going to be all week?'

'No! Oh no, Stewart.' In her relief the words came out too quickly, too fervently. 'I've been doing some thinking. We have to stay here because those are Jarrod's terms and he won't change them. But we'll keep away from him. Do our own thing. Starting this morning.'

For the first time the tightness in Stewart's face lightened. He looked absurdly relieved. Cathy felt an odd stab of guilt at the sight. Stewart was like a little boy she thought, who had been behaving truculently because he was not sure of his position.

'Do you really mean that?' he asked.

'Of course.'

She reached up and kissed him, holding her body against his for a long moment. As her lips were pressed to his it came to her that she had taken the initiative a few times in the last two days—each time in an effort to reassure him—and herself. The thought bothered her.

Withdrawing from him, she took a step away. She could not meet his eyes. She was scared that he would read in them something he would not like. She said, 'We'll go out in your car today. Jarrod said we should look on the week as a holiday—we'll do just that.'

Stewart pushed his hand through his hair. 'It won't be a holiday with him around.'

'He won't be with us. We'll go alone, and I'll show you the park.' She smiled up at him. 'I'll show you things you might never spot on your own.'

'All right.' He smiled at her for the first time that morning. 'How do we begin?'

'With breakfast,' she told him, keeping up the show of cheerfulness.

His face was wary. 'Breakfast with Jarrod?'

'By ourselves. I'm going round to the kitchen to see what I can find. How do scrambled eggs and sausages sound to you?'

'Just fine.' The smile had reached his eyes. 'While you make breakfast I'll go and make a 'phone-call.'

'Doug Jansen?'

'Right. The boss has to know that our plans have changed and that I won't be at the office on Monday.'

'I'll have to get word back, too. Mrs Fairchild's bedroom will be delayed another week, poor soul.' She gestured. 'Use the 'phone in Jarrod's office. He won't mind, and it's unlikely he'll be there this time of the morning.'

On her way to the kitchen Cathy reflected that

today's outing would serve more than one purpose. It was a way of killing time away from Jarrod and the compound, as well as a means of appeasing Stewart and showing him that all she wanted was to be with him. But it was more than that. It was a gesture of defiance. A challenge to Jarrod. A way of telling him that she would not let him get to her, no matter that he might think otherwise.

But Jarrod was nowhere to be seen. Neither was Amos. Enquiries addressed to the camp staff elicited no more than that the two men had gone out together very early, at the first light of dawn. Where they had gone or why was not known. So much for her independent gesture, Cathy thought. As she selected the eggs and began to whip them to a froth, she tried to push aside a tiny frisson of disquiet.

Breakfast was almost ready when Stewart joined her, a frown between his brows. 'Couldn't get hold of Doug,' he complained.

'That's too bad,' Cathy sympathised. 'But it's only Saturday, he's sure to be in sooner or later.'

'I'll try again later. One way or another I have to let him know what's happening.'

'You could even speak to him tomorrow.'

'A bit late. For me to be back in the office on Monday we'd have to be leaving Marakizi no later than noon tomorrow.'

'Well, don't worry about Doug now,' Cathy soothed. 'Eventually you'll find him in, and I so much want you to enjoy the day.'

'I mean to enjoy it.' Stewart took the cup of coffee she held out to him. 'Jarrod not joining us?'

'He's not in the compound.' The lightness in Cathy's tone concealed her uneasiness.

Stewart's face brightened. 'Fantastic. Now I know I will enjoy myself.'

It was still early. The sun was not yet high in the

sky, but already the slanting rays that came from the east brought a lovely warmth that later would turn to a blazing heat. While Cathy and Stewart ate, small blue birds, their feathers jewel-bright, hopped and fluttered everywhere, fighting for the crumbs which the two humans let drop. Cathy watched them, her mouth curving in an unconscious smile.

'One gets so used to a place,' she observed as she watched a bird, quicker than the others, pick at a piece of crust that Stewart had thrown to the ground. 'These birds, for instance, I used to take them for granted. It's only now, that I'm back, that I realise how much they're a part of Marakizi.'

'You've been remembering things ever since yesterday, haven't you?' Stewart asked quietly.

She looked at him, caught by something in his tone, then averted her eyes. 'I have,' she admitted.

She'd been remembering more than he could realise, she thought a while later, as they drove slowly along the sandy roads of the game-park. Here and there they saw animals, and they were *her* animals. Around the next bend they would come upon a clump of acacias, and a hundred yards further there would be a patch of dead, ghost-like trees. Every turn in the road was familiar. Almost she could have walked it blindfold.

'The drought has left its mark,' she said sadly, as they crossed a bridge and she looked down at a dry river-bed.

'The last three years have been bad everywhere in Africa,' Stewart said.

'They've been devastating. Jarrod has done what he could. You must have noticed the windmills? The bridge we just crossed, Stewart, there used to be so much water in the stream. There's not a drop left.'

'Do you see everything only in terms of Marakizi?' Stewart asked impatiently.

'I hope not. But Marakizi is my home. It . . .' She bit her lip, her cheeks flushing suddenly as she understood what she had said.

'I'm sorry,' she said uncertainly, with a look at Stewart's face.

'It's obviously the way you feel,' he said flatly.

'No! Oh Stewart, I really am sorry. It should never have come out the way it did.'

'You see this place as your home.'

'It isn't home. Not any longer. It will never be home again.' Feeling stripped and raw, she stopped, striving for composure, seeing by his expression that he did not believe her. And she knew, suddenly, that she had nothing to apologise for, that she was trying too hard. Her voice level now, she went on, 'But it was home once. I can't change that.'

'I see.'

'I don't think you do.' She turned to him, an unconscious plea in her voice, her eyes, in the little gesture of her hands. 'You'll see once you're in Canada. There will be a part of you that will always have roots in Africa. And that won't mean a confusion of loyalties. It's just . . . just the way it will be.'

'And Jarrod?' Stewart's voice was tight. It was as if her pleading had meant nothing to him.

'I wish you'd forget Jarrod.'

'Will there be a part of you that will always think of him as your husband?' he went on relentlessly.

No. The word trembled on her lips, and stopped there unuttered. She looked at him in confusion, wondering why the word was so difficult to say.

'Only as an ex-husband,' she said at last carefully.

'I'd like to think that's true.'

Her nails clenched in her hands. Both men were putting her through an emotional mangle, each in his own way, and she did not know how much more she could take of it.

'I've told you it is.' Her voice throbbed with hopelessness and despair. 'I don't know how to convince you. You just have to believe me.'

Whether it was her words or the intensity of emotion in her voice, Cathy had no way of telling. Perhaps Stewart just realised that there was a point beyond which it became unwise to pursue the issue. He took one of her hands in his and stroked it gently. 'I do believe you,' he said. 'We came out here to enjoy ourselves. Let's concentrate on the countryside.'

'Let's,' she agreed over the unshed tears in her throat.

Very slowly, because it was the only way to proceed through game country, they made their way along the winding road. Stewart was at the wheel. Cathy sat with her face averted from him, scouring the bush for animals. She was glad he couldn't see her expression, for she knew it was still strained, that her eyes were over-bright. She needed a while to regain her composure.

By the time she saw the wart-hogs she had herself under control once more.

'Stewart, look,' she said softly.

'Where . . .?' He drew the car to a halt, frowning as he followed the direction of her gesturing hand.

'There, in the bushes. See them?'

'No . . . Why, yes! Good God, how did you spot them?'

So much better did she feel by now that she was actually able to laugh at his astonishment. 'Years of training.'

'They're the same colour as the bush.'

'Camouflage. Nature's way of protecting her creatures.'

'Amazing! I'd never have seen them.'

'They're hoping the predators won't see them

either. But if there is danger that male—do you see him, the big one?—will throw up his tail as a sign of danger to the others.'

They were silent a few moments as they watched the little animals make their awkward way through the bush, and then Cathy pointed to the branches of a tree. 'Another tidbit ... Hear the birds?'

The car windows were open. Stewart sat quite still, listening. At last he said, 'Yes.'

'A territorial warning.'

'What does that mean?'

She laughed. 'One bird warning another of its territorial limits.'

'And the birds understand each other?'

'Oh yes.'

'And you understand too.' He peered at her. 'This is a new side of you, Cathy. Are you some kind of Doctor Doolittle?'

She laughed again, at ease for the first time that morning. 'I don't pretend to be able to speak to the animals. But there are things I understand. Things I know.'

Momentarily she held her breath. But Stewart didn't remark that Marakizi was in her soul, didn't question whether Jarrod understood the veld as she did—and she was able to relax once more.

Stewart was a dear, she thought, as they drove on once more. It would be too much to expect of any man that he would be impervious to the under-currents at Marakizi, or that he would not resent his future wife's affinity with the place. But he was making the best of a hateful situation, and by and large he was doing it graciously. I'm lucky to have him, she told herself with a glance at the good-looking profile. He turned, and as their eyes met and held she put a quick hand over his on the wheel, and he smiled.

After that things were better between them. They

drove further, stopping here and there to watch an animal, and Stewart was fascinated with all he saw. The elephant no more than ten yards from the roadside, snapping a branch just as easily as if it was a twig. The herd of zebra—he was intrigued by the fact that no two zebra were exactly alike, that their markings were as individual as human finger-prints. The monkeys swinging from the branches of a sausage-tree, and the baboons carrying their young with all the solemnity of young mothers wheeling their babies in a city park.

Stewart switched off the engine of the car when they came upon the giraffe. Cathy opened the window which she had closed a few minutes earlier to block the baboon which would have reached in and scalped her, and looked her fill at the animals she loved so much. It was an idyllic scene, two giraffe nibbled at the leaves of a tall acacia, their lovely coats glowing in the sun that slanted through the trees. When a hand reached out and took one of Cathy's she did not turn. Her eyes were on the giraffe, taking in every detail, storing the picture they made in her mind.

'I thought you'd be relaxed,' Stewart said.

'I am.'

'Your fingers aren't.' He laughed. 'I believe they're itching to get hold of a sketching-pencil.'

She turned in her seat, laughing back at him. 'How well you know me.' She looked at him, and saw that his expression was calm and unthreatened. It was safe to speak her thoughts. 'I really would love to sketch them.'

'Do these giraffe have transmitters?'

'Perhaps. It's hard to tell without binoculars.'

After a moment Stewart said, 'What's the purpose of Jarrod's work?'

'The love of research.' She paused, then went on. 'Does that seem very strange to you?'

Stewart shifted in his seat. 'It does. Is there money to be made with this work?'

'Not very much.'

'Then why? I mean, Marakizi must cost a fortune to maintain.'

'Jarrod is a rich man, Stewart. You haven't seen the lodges. They're really successful business ventures.'

'Perhaps I don't understand.' Stewart frowned. 'Why does he bury himself in this lonely place? What is the fascination with giraffe?'

'He doesn't regard it as a form of burial. There are men who climb mountain peaks. If you were to ask them why, they'd say because the peaks are there. Jarrod is a little like that. He has money, Stewart, and he's worked very hard for it. But he needs more than financial success to be happy.' After a moment she went on simply, 'It's just the way he is.'

'I see.'

Because she had a notion that he did not see at all, and that she could not help him, Cathy began to talk about the giraffe. She told him of the things Jarrod had learned, explained how the transmitters were able to relay vital information even when the animals themselves were far from the compound.

'You know so much about everything,' Stewart commented at last.

'It was my work,' she said simply.

'Decorating is your work now.' Was that a hint of sharpness in Stewart's tone?

'It is, and I love it,' she said lightly.

Some of the joy had gone from the scene. It was time to leave, before the pleasure the giraffe had given her was soured.

'It's hot,' she said. 'Why don't we drive on?'

Stewart's look told her that he was not taken in by the gambit she'd used to end the discussion. 'We'll be working together,' he said.

She met his gaze. 'I'm looking forward to it. Oh Stewart, I really am looking forward to it.'

They drove on then, and Cathy wished that she could dispel the leaden feeling within her. She had tried so hard to put on a show of cheerfulness, but it was difficult to convince Stewart when she could not convince herself that she was happy.

And then Stewart asked, 'How did you meet Jarrod?'

CHAPTER SEVEN

CATHY kept her eyes on the scenery. 'Why do you persist in torturing yourself?'

'I'm interested. You're going to be my wife, darling. I can't help wondering what drew you to a man like Jarrod.'

I couldn't help being drawn to him, she wanted to say. It was as inevitable as the day that follows night.

'We met at a lecture. Jarrod was giving a talk on wild-life research, his topic was the work that he was doing at the time. I was deeply interested. After the lecture I went to talk to him.'

She was silent, remembering. He had been so tall and tanned and handsome. Not a woman in the room had not been touched by his charisma, by the sheer force of his sexuality, she could swear to it. Cathy had been no exception. He had spoken to her about the newest developments in the field, and she had concentrated hard on giving intelligent responses. And all the while there had been a tautness in her stomach and an awareness that made her legs feel like jelly.

'He asked me to have dinner with him,' she said aloud. 'I accepted. That was the beginning.'

A few simple words to describe the start of their courtship. Words that made no attempt to describe the sexual tension that had been between them from the very beginning. Fireworks exploding on hot dry air, that was how it had been with them. Shattering, yet wonderful. Defying the image Cathy had had herself of a cool lady with an interest only in art and science.

'How long before you were married?'

'A few weeks.'

'A whirlwind courtship,' Stewart remarked drily.

She smiled at him. 'No more than ours. We haven't known each other any longer.'

But the time-factor was the only thing the two courtships had in common. Cathy, relatively untouched by men until she had met Jarrod, had fallen in love with a passion and a fierceness that had taken her completely by surprise. At nineteen she had been kissed by boyfriends, and had found the exercise pleasant enough, but she had never been tempted to go further. Sex was not the wonder it was made out to be, she had decided. She was happy to wait until marriage to experience the whole of it—and in no hurry for it at that.

Jarrod had shattered her illusions, had made nonsense of every smug theory she had ever held on the matter. Sensuous, masculine, devastatingly sexy, he had filled her body with a fire and a need that she had never dreamed existed. In his arms she had become passionate and abandoned, her untutored lips and hands making love to him with a desire she had not known was in her. He had carried her with him to such heights of sensation that her body had craved fulfilment.

The incredible, marvellous thing had been that he had wanted her as much as she had wanted him. That she had the power to affect this man, eleven years older than herself, handsome and an expert with women, had been a constant source of astonishment to her.

'Marry me tomorrow,' he had demanded after a week, his voice deep and husky with passion.

'Tomorrow is impossible.' Her whole being had been filled with happiness. 'A month, darling. My parents will want to make certain arrangements.'

'A month is too long,' he had groaned. And then,

'All right, I suppose I can wait that long. After all, we have forever ahead of us.'

Forever. Forever had lasted three years. And the undying love they had sworn each other had turned out to be, on Jarrod's side at least, no more than a physical infatuation. On Cathy's part it had been a much more genuine emotion, but it had died along with her baby.

'After the first novelty wore off life must have been boring for you here.'

At the sound of Stewart's words Cathy jerked. So lost had she been in her memories that for a while she had forgotten his very existence. Blinking her eyes, she looked at him, wondering what he meant.

'The days must have dragged.'

They had never dragged, and life had never been boring. Every day there had been new things to learn, new facts to discover. Her sketch-pencil had worked busily. There had been no time to be bored. And at night there had always been the wonder of their lovemaking, a passionate lovemaking whose excitement had never waned.

'It would have been rough on you, having a baby out here,' Stewart said reflectively. 'So far away from civilisation.'

'It's a lot more civilised now than it was a year ago,' Cathy said feelingly. 'The helicopter and the telephone, those are new. I wonder why Jarrod acquired them. Not that it matters. Not now . . .'

'Even with the 'phone you'd have been lonely.'

With a husband she could depend on she wouldn't have been lonely. People *en masse* had never been necessary for Cathy's happiness. But to be left quite alone when she had needed help so badly had been a shattering experience. The terror had lingered long after the event itself. For months after she had left Marakizi there had been nightmares. She was unable to forget the pain of labour and the sense of being alone with no way of getting to a hospital; the relief when the strangers, arriving unexpectedly, had rushed her to the nearest town; the despair upon learning that the baby had died, that it could have been saved if she'd been at the hospital earlier.

Even now, a year later, the nightmares still occurred. No longer every night. But no less intense than at the beginning, waking her every time in a state of perspiration and weeping.

There were things she would never forgive Jarrod. If he had given her more sheer joy than any other man before him—or after him if her suspicions were correct—he had also been the cause of more heart-wrenching unhappiness.

'I'll certainly be better off in Canada,' she said flatly.

Stewart looked at her through narrowed eyes. As if he sensed something of her thoughts, he said, 'You're no longer a starry-eyed nineteen-year-old, dazzled by a handsome man—Jarrod is handsome, I'll grant you that. You're almost four years older now, you must have different needs.'

'You don't have to convince me.' Her voice was harsh. 'I know every word of the script. I might have written it myself.'

Stewart was right. She was no longer the naïve girl Jarrod had married. Excitement, both in lovemaking and in their research, had once been enough for her. Not any more. The last months had shown her another side of herself. It had become important for her to have stability in her life. To have a husband whom she could depend on for more than the ability to arouse her body. She wanted children, a home, a career. She also wanted love.

With Stewart she would have all those things. If her body whispered that he could not fulfil her physically in the way that she wanted, she would ignore such treacherous whisperings. Marakizi had opened up wounds that were more raw than she had realised. But another few days and she would have left here, a few months and she could be in Canada. Stewart might not be perfect, but then the perfect man probably did not exist. And her new maturity had taught her the value of compromise.

At noon, when the sun blazed down from its full height and the animals rested listlessly in whatever shade they could find, Cathy and Stewart made their way back to the compound.

Jarrod had not returned, but the compound staff were unperturbed by his absence. It seemed that Jarrod had left instructions that his guests should eat without him. Obviously he had planned to be out all day.

It was infinitely more pleasant without him. And yet, as they sat down to a light lunch of sliced mangoes and pawpaw with ice-cream, Cathy found herself having to feign an appetite. Jarrod's work often took him away from the compound, there was nothing unusual in that. Yet Cathy felt again the disquiet she had experienced earlier in the day, and her throat was dry with tension.

They rested a while after lunch, Stewart in his room, Cathy in hers, Cathy having rejected, quite gently, Stewart's entreaties to join him. It was so burningly hot that a siesta was about the only way to pass the time, for Stewart in particular. He was not used to the heat, and he looked pale and exhausted.

It was only much later in the afternoon, when the sun was lower and moving west-wards, that they ventured out of doors once more. It was a good time for seeing animals. Or perhaps they were just very lucky. Even with her mind on other things, Cathy spotted the flash of movement in the bush, and snapped a swift order to Stewart to stop the car.

'Cheetah,' she said tersely, pointing with her hand.

'My God, you're right!'

'Look your fill, Stewart. It's a very rare sight.'

'And a beautiful one.' Stewart looked awed. 'Are the stories of a cheetah's speed exaggerated?'

'Not on your life!' Cathy laughed. 'Seventy-five miles per hour is a fair sprint.'

'Incredible!'

'It is rather, isn't it? On a hunt, it can only keep up that kind of speed for a quarter of a mile or so, but that's usually enough, for then the poor victim's been downed.' Cathy's eyes were on the cheetah. As with the giraffe earlier that day, she was committing every line of the sleek stream-lined body to memory. 'The irony is,' she went on, 'that after a high-speed chase the cheetah is exhausted. Then it's no big deal for a hyena, which is the stronger animal to begin with, to steal the bounty from under the cheetah's hungry nose.'

'That's hardly fair.'

'As with love, the survival game knows no fairness.'

She had said nothing intrinsically wrong, and yet Cathy regretted the words the moment she'd uttered them. Stewart's silence told her the remark had hit a sensitive spot. If she could have, she would have found a way of apologising, of telling him the statement had no bearing on their own situation—but she was aware that anything she might say would make things worse. It was almost a relief when the cheetah made a sudden move and vanished in the thick bush. It was time for the car to move on.

At a water-hole they stopped a while. Impala and zebra and wildebeest were drinking. The western sun slanted over the water, splintering its surface into a thousand topaz diamonds, and an air of tranquillity hung over the silent land.

Normally Cathy would have enjoyed the lovely twilight scene to the fullest. Yet while she watched the animals, while she talked to Stewart, part of her mind was with Jarrod. Where was he? When would he be back? Was he safe?

The jeep was not in its usual spot by the time they got back to camp. It was a fact which did not concern Stewart in the least. But Cathy looked anxiously at the empty spot, fear beginning to create a nasty taste in her dry mouth. Relax, she told herself. There's still some day-light left. And Jarrod knows how to look after himself.

But the fear remained.

'I'm off to try Doug again,' Stewart said. 'Hold thumbs that he'll be there this time.'

Cathy watched him walk away in the direction of Jarrod's office. In the compound preparations were being made for the night. Marakizi had its own electric generator, but now and then it was erratic, and kerosene lamps, cleaned and filled, were always at hand for use in the event of a power failure. One of the compound staff was carrying lamps into the bungalows, another was preparing the fire for the braaivleis.

The air of tranquillity which had been present at the water-hole, hung over the compound. That, and the special smell which was strong on the still air. A smell that was a composite of smoke and dust and trees and of the bushes of the veld. The man who laid the fire looked up suddenly and smiled, and Cathy smiled back, hiding her restlessness.

Where the hell was Jarrod?

Stewart came back, his feet crunching on the stone path. One look at his face told her he was troubled.

'No luck?' she queried.

'No. Well yes, in the sense that Doug was in this time. But I have to be back at the office on Monday.'

'Oh Stewart!' Cathy stared at him, her eyes suddenly wide. 'You know Jarrod's terms.'

'The bloody autocrat will have to go back on them,' Stewart said moodily.

Jarrod was an autocrat all right, but at this moment, tense with fear, she did not care to hear him described in that way. Still, she let the words go, as she said, 'Didn't you explain to Doug?'

'Sure, I tried. My boss has no sympathy with a difficult husband. Something's come up, and I'm needed at the office. Have to be there first thing Monday morning.'

'I see . . .'

'Jarrod will have to understand.'

'We'll talk to him when he comes.'

If he comes. The words sounded silently in Cathy's mind. She glanced at her watch. About fifteen minutes left until dark. As with the Kruger National Park, Jarrod had strict rules about driving after dark, for on unlit roads there was always the danger of animals being hit. Jarrod did not abuse the rules that he laid down for his guests.

The sun was setting quickly now. For some time the sky had been awash with the dramatic colours of the sunset. It was also starting to get chilly, for with the onset of night this part of the Lowveld grew very cold.

On the same premise that applies to a watched kettle refusing to boil, Cathy decided to go and change out of the shorts and blouse she had been wearing all day. Clad in cord trousers and a rose-pink angora sweater, she came out of her room to hear the sound of a car stopping. The jeep! She knew the sound so well that she did not have to see it to know that the jeep had returned.

With a gladness she did not stop to analyse, she hurried in its direction. Amos had got out of the vehicle, and Jarrod, who had been driving, was getting out too. Neither of the men saw Cathy. They were carrying guns, she saw without surprise. At the back of the vehicle they came together, and stood talking. On the silent air she could hear the low-pitched voices, but she was too far away to hear what they said.

'Jarrod! Amos!' she called.

They jerked round, surprised. Cathy saw the expression on their faces. Bone-weary frustration. But on Jarrod's face, at least, the expression was quickly masked.

Pleasantly he said, 'Hello, Cathy, have a good day?'

Impatiently she brushed the question aside. 'I was getting worried.'

'Why on earth should you have been worried?'

'You've been out all day. And it's so late.' She paused, biting her lip as she saw an impersonal blankness appear in Jarrod's eyes. *What I do is my business,* it seemed to say.

'Where were you?' she asked nevertheless.

'In the veld.'

'What were you doing?'

A look passed from Jarrod to Amos. The exchange lasted no more than a second, but Cathy, who knew them both so well, was able to read it. *We keep our own counsel.* That was the message that was passed wordlessly from one man to the other. Even before he opened his mouth, she knew that Jarrod was going to evade the question.

'Working,' he said briefly as Amos walked away.

Cathy took a step closer to Jarrod. She saw the strain beneath his eyes, the brown dust that layered his face. He was a grim and tired man, angry too.

She looked at him levelly. 'I think you went after the lion.'

After a moment, Jarrod said, 'That too.'

'With any success?'

'No.'

'It's not the first time, is it?'

'I've told you that already.'

'When was the first time, Jarrod?'

'I'm not in the mood for chit-chat, right now.' He sounded irritated and impatient.

'It's not chit-chat.'

'The lion is *my* business. You didn't know about it before you came here, it won't concern you one way or another once you're in Canada.'

'I want to know, Jarrod.'

'And I want a shower and a change of clothes.' His lips lifted in the travesty of a smile. 'I'll join you and Stewart at the fire.'

She watched him vanish into their—*his* bungalow. Her hands were clenched and her expression was tight. Damn you, Jarrod! She sent the words across the silent air. Damn you for treating me like this.

Gone was her fear. In its place was anger. Damn Jarrod for shutting her out of his life like this. As if she did not deserve to know what was happening here at Marakizi. He must take her for the worst kind of fool if he thought she did not know that the only reason he'd gone out today was the lion. She had been sure of it all day, though she had not wanted to acknowledge the cause of her fear. A marauding lion was a dangerous animal, and that it was still very much at large was evidenced by the frustration she had glimpsed in both men's faces.

Damn you, Jarrod, for not talking to me!

With quick angry steps she went to the fire and took the beer Stewart held out to her. 'I see Jarrod got back,' he said.

'Yes.'

'You seemed concerned about him.'

'Without justification,' she said shortly.

'We'll have to talk to him.'

'Yes . . .'

Stewart looked around him. 'I can't say I'll be

sorry to see the back of Marakizi. I was dreading the thought of a week in this place. I think we should leave before noon tomorrow, honey.'

She played with her glass. 'I suppose we should.'

In the fire-pit the flames were leaping, vivid orange against the gathering darkness. The crickets were beginning their nightly shrilling, and somewhere a frog croaked. And then, across the silent veld came the low trumpeting of an elephant. Stewart looked momentarily startled. Cathy reached out to touch his hand. She was smiling, but inside her, deep in her chest, there was a hollow sensation. Tomorrow at this time she might be well on her way to Johannesburg. There was a part of her that wanted to go. And there was another part that did not know how she would bear it.

The flames were lower by the time Jarrod joined the other two at the fire. He was a different man from the one who had arrived in the jeep. The dusty safari-suit had been replaced by well-cut brown trousers and a matching sweater which hugged the broad chest and revealed the thrust of a strong throat. His face was clean of dust, and his hair was still damp from his shower.

'Good, you've helped yourselves to drinks.' As he reached for a beer and opened it, his voice was relaxed.

And then the firelight caught his face, and Cathy saw that he was anything but relaxed. Something remained of the strain and the fatigue she had seen earlier, giving the hard-boned face with its straight mouth and chiselled jaw-line a touch of vulnerability. Cathy's anger vanished as she felt a tug at her heart-strings. He was so good-looking. Physically all that a man could be, intelligent and powerful and self-sufficient with it. Evidence of ordinary human frailty in such a man was almost unbearably poignant.

Quite involuntarily she took a step towards him.

Her hand was lifting, about to touch him, to stroke the strain and the fatigue from that splendid face. And then reality hit, and she dropped her hand, appalled.

Dimly she heard Stewart say, 'Jarrod . . .' At the tone in his voice she turned, realising what he was about to say. Surely he must understand that this was the wrong time! Jarrod was staring moodily into his drink, making it safe for Cathy to touch a quick hand to Stewart's at the same time as she shook her head. 'Later,' she mouthed. Later, when Jarrod had eaten, when he'd had a chance to unwind, that would be the time to tell him that they were leaving Marakizi.

Jarrod looked up. 'You were saying?'

'We . . .' Stewart hesitated and Cathy held her breath. 'We saw a cheetah.'

'Marvellous. Cathy must have told you it's a rare sight.'

'She did indeed.'

The conversation became easy and general. Stewart talked about the animals they had seen, and Jarrod, once more the genial host, was responsive to the point of supplying some entertaining anecdotes. Stewart did not mention the change in plans, Jarrod did not volunteer information about his doings that day.

We're all acting, Cathy thought.

It was only later, when the meal was over and Jarrod had tossed a fresh log on the fire, that Stewart said, 'We have to talk.'

Jarrod turned a pleasant face. 'What about?'

He knows, Cathy thought tensely. He's known all the time.

'Cathy and I are leaving here tomorrow.'

'Splendid.'

The one word must have caught Stewart by surprise because he looked uncertain of himself. 'I spoke to my boss. I have to be back at the office on Monday.'

Apart from a lifted eyebrow there was no response from Jarrod. Stewart said, 'That being the case you'll have to give us your consent no later than tomorrow morning.'

Again Jarrod made no response.

Looking slightly unnerved now, Stewart said, 'I take it, that will be in order.'

'No.' Jarrod's tone was still pleasant.

'But I've just explained.' Stewart was beginning to sound belligerent. 'You must have understood.'

'Perfectly.'

'Stop playing with us,' Cathy said sharply.

'I'm not playing.'

'For God's sake, Jarrod!' She was very angry now. 'You know exactly what you're doing.'

'Naturally. I'm sticking to my terms.' He paused before saying meaningfully. 'Just as you knew I would.'

She *had* known it, of course. She'd known it from the moment Stewart had given her the news, though she'd tried to convince herself otherwise.

The shrilling of the crickets had grown louder. In the fire-pit the new flames crackled and danced. A few moths hovered around the kerosene lamp that was suspended from the branch of a nearby tree. Once more the elephant trumpeted, but this time Cathy was too tense to feel emotion. It was a tension which was echoed in Stewart who sat so close beside her that she could feel the corded stiffness of his body.

'You can't do this to us!' Stewart burst out at last.

Jarrod had poured himself another beer. He was staring into its depths, as if fascinated by the flames reflected in the liquid.

'For God's sake, man, don't you have anything to say?'

Jarrod looked at Stewart. 'What is there to say?'

'That you'll give us the consent.'

'You already know the answer to that.' It was said with a touch of deliberate weariness.

This time the weariness did nothing to Cathy's emotions. 'Stewart's boss is depending on him.'

'I believe you.'

'Stop stringing us along. What do you suggest we do?'

'You know the choices. I don't think I have to spell them out to you.' Jarrod sounded amused.

'I don't have a choice,' Stewart said. 'I have to go back.'

'It's Cathy who has to stay the week,' Jarrod said.

There was a moment of silence while the remark made its impact.

Stewart swore then, using a word Cathy had never heard him utter before. 'Out of the question. She's not staying here without me.'

'That makes my consent out of the question as well,' Jarrod said.

'It's what you'd like, isn't it,' Stewart was bitter. 'Cathy all to youself for a week. Give you a chance to insinuate yourself with her. Spread your poison. Get her to come back to you.'

'He wouldn't have a chance,' Cathy declared over the sudden beating of her heart.

Jarrod laughed, setting fire to her raw nerves. 'I think you're both making some assumptions.'

He was a cruel man when he wanted to be. And such an expert at knowing how to hurt her.

'Why do you want her here a week then?' Stewart demanded.

'I don't intend to discuss the reason,' was the only rejoinder.

Deadlock. Stewart clearly felt as frustrated as she did, Cathy thought. All his frustration was in his voice when he said, 'For arrogance you must take some beating.'

'My wife would agree with you.' Jarrod did not seem in the least offended.

'A hundred-fold,' Cathy said quietly. 'I mean to marry Stewart, so I'll stay behind when he goes. But be warned, my presence will give you no joy. You'll be relieved when the week is over.'

'I daresay I will.' Jarrod got to his feet. He stood against the flames, a tall lithe figure, dangerous as the lion that roamed his territory, and as ruthless. 'I'm off to bed, it's been a long day. Stay by the fire as long as you wish, but see that it's put out before you leave it.'

'Another order,' Stewart muttered sullenly.

Jarrod grinned, infuriating them both. 'If that's how you choose to regard it. Will I see you before you go, Stewart?'

'Unfortunately.'

'Then I'll just say good night.'

Without waiting for their responses, knowing perfectly well none would be forthcoming, he vanished into the night.

'Bastard,' Stewart said feelingly, when he had gone.

'We should have known . . .'

'Doesn't he understand?'

'Jarrod has never been short on intelligence,' Cathy said bitterly.

'Then why, Cathy, why?'

'The same reason all along. He knows it will be hell for me to be here.'

'Will it be hell?'

Cathy pushed at the soft sand with the toe of her shoe. 'Yes.'

Stewart pulled her against him, and she made no effort to resist. His lips covered her face with tiny kisses, then buried themselves in her hair. 'I hate this.' The words were muffled.

'I do too.'

'The week will be eternity.'

'But it will end,' she tried to soothe him.

He drew away to look down at her. 'There must be a way of getting round him.'

'Not once he's made up his mind.'

'I still think he wants you back.'

Cathy drew a painful breath. 'He's hardly acting the loving husband.'

'Perhaps not. What about you, honey?' He peered down at her, his voice quietly desperate as he went on, 'Do you think you could be persuaded to go back to him?'

'You know how I feel.'

He held her very tightly. His arms were warm and comforting and infinitely pleasant. But nothing more, she thought, a little despairingly.

At last he said, 'Will this week be a torment for you too, Cathy?'

'Oh yes,' she said. And she knew that that at least was true.

They did not linger long by the fire. Through it was to be their last evening together for a while, the flames had lost their appeal, and the air was cold. Stewart seemed strangely pre-occupied, and Cathy did not object when he rose to extinguish the flames.

'My poor Stewart,' she said as they made their way to the guest-rooms. 'This is all more than you bargained for.'

'It is,' he agreed.

She hesitated. Then she suggested, 'Shall I come to your room tonight?'

They had reached the adjoining rooms, and he had a hand on the door-handle of the leopard-room. She heard him drew breath as he turned towards her. Then he said, 'No, darling, I don't think so.'

She wound her arms around his waist. 'I want to.'

'Not tonight. I may be all sorts of a fool, Cathy . . .' He stopped and cupped her face with his hands. When he went on his voice had grown harder. 'Last night I would have leaped to accept what you're offering. Now ... Cathy darling, let's get this week over with, then we'll have a life of loving ahead of us.'

He kissed her, sweetly, but without passion. And then he went into the room and shut the door behind him.

CHAPTER EIGHT

AT the knock Jarrod called, 'Come in, Cathy,' She pushed open the door—the way she felt she would have liked to give it a good kick—and she knew that he had used her name deliberately.

'You knew I would come.' Her cheeks were flushed and she was breathing fast as she stood in the open doorway. Jarrod was in bed, the sheet was drawn up to just beneath his armpits, and the bathroom light shed just enough of a glow to reveal a bare throat and shoulders. Evidently Jarrod had not changed his custom of sleeping naked.

A little pulse jerked in Cathy's own throat as she took a breath. She could *not* let Jarrod's sensuous appeal affect her now.

He grinned, and she sensed that the glance that took in her slender form, seeing beneath the jeans and the soft sweater to the breasts and thighs and hips which in the past had trembled beneath his touch, was pure insolence. 'Yes, I knew.'

'Then you also know why I'm here.'

'To plead your case,' he declared lazily.

'Wrong. I know I'd be wasting my time.'

Surprise showed for a moment in the dark eyes, to be replaced by a look of such outrageous speculation that she stiffened, fighting to control both her composure and her temper.

'You want me to make love to you.'

'Wrong again,' she got out through dry lips. 'What an arrogant man you are, Jarrod, Stewart was right about that. You think of yourself as God's gift to women, and to me in particular.' Lifting her chin, she threw him a look of pure challenge. 'It may interest you to know that before I came in here I asked Stewart to sleep with me.'

Something moved in his jaw, but the glint in his eyes was unchanged. 'And he didn't satisfy you? My poor frustrated Cathy. What does it feel like to go from one man's bed to another because you didn't get the satisfaction you wanted?'

'You really are despicable. I didn't sleep with Stewart.'

'He turned you down? Does the man have water in his veins?'

'He has honour. Something you don't know the meaning of.'

Jarrod laughed, his teeth showing white against his skin. 'From the look of you it would seem that honour doesn't keep you fulfilled.'

'I'd say it promises very well for our future life together.'

'He must know you're not a virgin.'

'Of course.'

'But he means to wait until you're married to make love to you? Isn't that carrying chivalry a bit far?'

'Who said anything about waiting?' she lied. 'Stewart and I are lovers already; but you know we'd decided to sleep apart at Marakizi.' Did the words hurt? she wondered. 'Our lovemaking will be all the sweeter when we know that I'm free.'

'Splendid,' he said lazily. 'I take it you're here to deliver some kind of ultimatum.'

'Right. I'll stay the week, Jarrod, I don't have any option. But I want you to promise not to touch me.'

He looked amused. 'Are you kidding?'

She bit her lip. This was even more difficult than she had feared. She wished that the sight of the bronzed body beneath the sheets did not have such an unnerving effect on her.

'You'd be taking unfair advantage of me,' she got out.

'Very likely.'

'It's not as if you still love me.' The words came out with some difficulty.

He did not reply immediately, and she found that she was holding her breath. He could deny the statement, even now he could deny it. And if he did, what would she do then? Oddly, she wasn't sure.

The words she awaited did not come. Instead he thrust aside the sheet and swung himself out of bed in one fluid movement. There was a moment when Cathy could have made it out of the door. But for two whole seconds her lungs stopped their breathing, and her brain was unable to send the correct message to her legs. By the time she was able to move once more it was too late. Jarrod was beside her, and somehow, whether by accident or design he had managed to insert himself between Cathy and the door.

After one compulsive glance Cathy averted her eyes. There was no light where they stood, but she did not need one. She had seen enough of the splendid body in that one stolen second to send the fire racing through her loins. What she could not see of him in the dim light memory supplied.

Jarrod's hands gripped her shoulders. 'Love! Who's talking of love? You're a beautiful woman, Cathy. You're sexy and desirable. While you're on my territory I'll take every chance I want to make love to you.'

She felt a little dizzy. 'I won't stand for it.'

'Oh you won't?' Hands still on her shoulders, he pulled her against him. It was not an embrace, and yet she was aware of every inch of the powerful body so close to hers.

She closed her eyes, seeking to deny what was happening, praying for some measure of a sanity that was fast disappearing.

'Did you think I was some knight in shining armour like your honourable Stewart?' Jarrod's voice was hard, mocking.

'I hoped ...'

His hands left her shoulders and slid to her back. Bending his head, he let his lips rest against the hollow in her throat. 'What did you hope?' he whispered softly.

'Not for this,' she gasped. Her hands went to his arms, meaning to push him away, and yet managing only to pull him closer against her. 'Not this, Jarrod.' Somehow she tilted back her head so that she could look at him. 'I don't want this!'

'We both do.' He was watching her, the lids heavy over his eyes, making it difficult to read them.

'This ... it's just sex. Was it always just sex, Jarrod?'

'You know what it was.' His voice had a bleak sound.

'Did you ever love me?'

He laughed, and his warm breath fanned her face. 'So like a woman. Love. Love is all you can think of.'

'I used to think that you loved me. And then ...'

The amusement left his face. 'We had a damn good sex-life, Cathy.'

All the time they'd been talking, she had been totally aware of the naked body just centimetres from her own. Had been aware of the long strong thighs, the hard chest where the quickened heart-beat throbbed in unison with her own. On one level of her mind had been the need to concentrate on what they both were saying, knowing that she had to parry his barbed comments with matching ones of her own. But on another level, a level that seemed to be purely female, sensuous and primitive, there had been the craving for a fulfilment that only his lovemaking could give her.

But his last words had hurt, knifing her to the depths of her being. It was as if he had cheapened everything that had been between them. Three wonderful years were suddenly reduced to nothing more than a physical thrill.

'You've touched me for the last time,' she said through gritted teeth.

'Wrong, darling.'

The hands which had never broken contact with her while they were talking, pushed suddenly to her hips, pulling her against him in an abrupt movement. She opened her mouth to protest, but the words were stilled by the lips that covered hers. There was nothing tender or loving in this kiss. It was hard and hungry, seeking something which she would not give him.

'Let me go,' she gasped outraged, when he lifted his head for breath.

'No.'

'You're hurting me.'

'I'm not hurting you, and you're loving it.' His eyes glittered down into hers. 'Ready for more, darling?'

'Kiss me and you'll be sorry,' she threw back at him.

In this mood of Jarrod's her words were like a red flag to a bull. Clearly he did not believe her. Well, there were other ways of showing him what she meant. In the moment when his mouth closed on hers, she bit him.

His head snapped back in shock, but even then he did not let go of her. 'You've become a hell-cat since we've been apart.'

'Oh, yes.' Let him know that he could not do as he pleased.

'Or perhaps,' he said softly, 'you're just very frustrated. Perhaps this is what you've been waiting for.'

He did not wipe away the drop of blood that had formed on his lip. Instead he bent to kiss her again. She made herself rigid, bracing herself for his undoubted punishment, but his kiss was the opposite of what she had been expecting. Erotically playful, tantalising, it drove an even hotter fire through her body.

'Have you kissed the blood away?' he whispered, and she saw that his lips were clean.

She was unable to answer him, but it seemed that he expected no answer, because he was bending to her again. In the time they'd spent apart his lips had not forgotten which were the most sensitive areas. Unerringly they sought out the arch of her throat, the little hollows beneath her ears, the soft skin around her eyes and her temples.

It was becoming harder and harder to resist him. She had been so determined not to let herself respond to him, but the determination was being swamped by a yearning to feel every inch of his flesh against her own.

This time when he kissed her mouth there was no holding back. She opened her lips to him, and her arms went around his neck, hands burying themselves in the thick dark hair that grew there.

There had been dreams during the time they'd been apart. Fevered dreams, in which Jarrod had made fierce love to her. Dreams from which she'd woken, to lie tormented and restless for the rest of the night, trying in vain to forget the visions her unconscious mind had thrown before her, knowing that the particular rapture she had enjoyed with Jarrod would never be hers to experience again. But she was awake now. Jarrod's lips, relentlessly erotic, were no dream, and she was unable to resist them. Did not have the will to resist them. Just as she had no will to resist the hands that undressed her, sliding the clothes from her body with familiar expertise.

And then his hands were caressing her body, relearning the shape of her hips and her waist, the soft swelling curves of her breasts. There was nothing hurried in his movements, it was the very slowness which made them all the more exciting. He was holding himself back with an exquisite control, seducing her with every touch as he let her breasts mould themselves into his hands, caressing the nipples with his long fingers, then touching his lips to the places where his fingers had been. Her body arched towards his, craving the fulfilment that only he could give her, and from her throat surged a moan of pleasure.

Even her dreams had never been like this. She had forgotten the depths of her own sensuality and passion, had forgotten how Jarrod could make her lose herself in him. His lips and his tongue and his body were bringing back the memories that she had tried to push from her. Every nerve and fibre of her being was alive, and wanting him.

'Stay with me tonight,' he whispered.

She stared at him through passion-glazed eyes, hearing what he said, but taking a few moments to understand. Slowly, very slowly, her thinking mind began to function once more, and her eyes dilated with horror.

'Stewart,' she gasped.

'He'll never know.'

'That's not the point,' she said on a sob, and tried to push away from him.

'Don't go, darling. Let me love you.' His arms tightened around her once again, lifting her, and she saw his eyes go to the bed.

'Jarrod, no!'

'It's been so long, Cathy.'

'Oh God, Jarrod, this should never have happened. I blame myself for letting it get out of hand.'

'Cathy . . .'

'Let me go, Jarrod. Oh damn you, let me stand.' The words came out in a voice that was choked with frustration and despair.

'Even though you want me.'

'That has nothing to do with it.'

He dropped her abruptly to the floor. His breathing was ragged, and she knew that he was as frustrated as she was.

'You're damned too, my darling wife,' he said, his voice hard. 'But I won't force you, unwilling ladies were never my scene. I've never yet had to force a woman to get what I wanted from her.'

How many women had there been in recent months? Enough, Cathy thought, and closed her eyes briefly to hide the treacherous rush of pain.

'Well, I am unwilling,' she said, making her voice as hard as she could.

'You weren't a few minutes ago.'

'I am now,' was all she could say.

He watched as she pulled on her clothes with shaking hands. 'I can see it will be quite a week,' he said at last.

She lifted her chin, the words coming from her lips almost as the decision was formed. 'I won't be here.'

'Really?' His voice was impassive.

'I'll be leaving tomorrow.'

The long body, relaxed in its nudity, did not change. 'Without the consent?'

'Yes.'

'As you wish.' A shrug of the shoulders. 'I'm mildly interested. Does this mean you're kissing Stewart farewell?'

'You are voraciously interested. I don't know

anything about immigration regulations, but if I can, I'll be going to Canada with Stewart.'

'As his mistress?'

'Right.'

She wished it was less dark where they stood, so that she could make out at least something of Jarrod's expression. 'And that will give you happiness?' he asked after a moment.'

'Not as much as if we were married.' Her voice held a challenge. 'But I won't be a mistress for long, Jarrod.'

'No?'

'You're a physical man. You won't be content to live alone for long. You'll find yourself a woman, and given the isolation of Marakizi you'll have to marry her if you want her to stay with you.' Her voice was fierce, yet pitched low to conceal the pain her own words caused her. 'You'll be the one knocking at my door for a divorce, Jarrod.'

'You have it all worked out,' he said coolly.

'You're right about that.' She managed to match his coolness. Then she walked out of the bungalow and closed the door firmly behind her.

Surprisingly, it was Stewart who resisted the idea. Dismayed, Cathy watched him as his expression grew remote. 'No go,' he said.

'You're rejecting me?' she asked in astonishment.

'I'm rejecting your idea. I don't want a mistress.'

'It's second best.' Her hands went out in a little gesture of pleading.

'Only the best is good enough for me. I want you to be my wife.'

'You're asking the impossible.' She tried to ignore the little shiver of apprehension.

'Not at all. Jarrod said he would give us the consent.'

'You know his terms.'

'And we agreed to them. You'll have to stay on here, Cathy.'

She stared at him, wondering at this new aloof Stewart, at a firmness she had never suspected. After a moment she said, 'But I hate the thought of it.'

His hands went to her shoulders, holding them tightly, and she winced a little, because the soft skin was still sensitive from Jarrod's lovemaking.

'Do you think I like it?' Stewart demanded.

'Then . . . then why?'

'I want to be married to you. Jarrod made himself very clear last night. Do you think he's likely to change his mind?'

Miserably she said, 'No.' And then, remembering the words she had thrown at Jarrod, that he would be the one who'd plead for a divorce, she amended, 'At least not yet.'

'Then there's no option.'

'Last night you were so adamant that you didn't want me staying here. Alone . . .' Her voice quivered just as little. 'Alone with Jarrod.'

'I've done a lot of thinking since then.'

There was something strange in his voice. In his eyes. Come to think of it, his manner was in no way that of the man she thought she'd come to know.

'Stewart . . .' She met his eyes, found she could not hold the gaze, and looked away.

'Are you scared to be with Jarrod?' he asked. Scared stiff. Petrified. Oh Stewart, you don't know how scared I am. Not because of what he might do to me. Jarrod would never hurt me, not physically. I'm scared of myself. Of what *I* might do. Of how I might react.

'Don't be silly,' she said stiffly.

'Cathy, look at me.'

She could not. At that moment she could not.

'Look at me!'

Slowly, reluctantly, she dragged her eyes back to his. The scrutiny he subjected her to was intent. She tried to remain relaxed and unconcerned, and thought she managed quite well in the circumstances. But as his gaze went to her lips she thought he could see the bruising beneath the lip-gloss, as it went to her eyes she knew he could see the despair that was so difficult to conceal.

Had Stewart come to her room again last night? If so, he would not have needed much imagination to guess her whereabouts. And one look at her face now would confirm any suspicions he might have had about what she had been doing.

Deliberately he asked, 'Will you want to sleep with Jarrod?'

'No!' The one word was choked.

He looked at her for another long moment. 'Be sure of that, darling.'

'Then you really want me to stay.' Somehow Cathy dragged out the words.

'Yes.' His face was sombre, but his expression was that of a man who had made up his mind. 'When you come to me, Cathy, I want you to be quite sure that Jarrod has no place in your life.'

Which is why you're throwing me in the lion's den. Putting me to the strongest test you can devise.

Two days they had been at Marakizi, and in that time Jarrod had shown her a side of him she had never known. Now she was seeing a new side of Stewart. It was strange, Cathy thought, just when you thought you knew someone, you discovered that you really did not know him at all.

She drew a small shuddering breath. Stewart cupped her face in his hands and bent to drop a kiss on her trembling mouth.

'See you Saturday,' he said softly. 'Take care of yourself, my darling.'

And with that Cathy had to be content. She wondered whether Stewart was wiser than she had realised. Either that, or he was incredibly foolish.

Stewart left some time before noon. Jarrod shook his hand, and Cathy clung to him a moment. 'The days will crawl by,' she said when she had kissed him, not caring that Jarrod heard her. Stewart held her tightly against him a moment, then drew away and got into the car.

Cathy stood at the gates of the compound and watched him drive away, tears gathering in her eyes as the car became smaller and smaller, merging at length with the dust cloud on the road.

Only when the last of the dust had settled did Cathy turn away from the gates. She walked back into the grounds of the compound. Silence had fallen. A heavy silence, the sounds of the veld notwithstanding.

Walking along the stony path, Cathy felt ill at ease. She wasn't sure where she was going. Didn't know what she wanted to do. Didn't even know what there *was* to do.

Once this had been her home. Then the days had been so filled with activity that she had wished sometimes for the gift of an extra hour or two. Now things were different. She couldn't walk into Jarrod's lab and work on his projects, doubtless he would have something to say if she did. She couldn't go into the kitchen and bake, something she had always loved doing. Or yes, theoretically speaking she could bake. Nobody would stop her. But she would feel uncomfortable. As if she was making a statement to the effect that this was once more *her* kitchen. The ramifications of such a statement—untrue as it would be—were such that she would rather not make it in the first place.

All of which left her where? With five and a half

days to spend—how? So many hours to kill. Wryly she wondered how much of that time would be spent avoiding Jarrod. Because she meant to avoid him. There would be no repetition of last night's love-scene.

'Well,' said the object of her thoughts, 'feel like coming for a drive with me later on?'

So absorbed had she been in her thoughts that she had not heard him come up behind her. 'No,' she answered disagreeably.

'Come and have lunch.'

'I'm not hungry.'

'Have a nice day,' he said equably and walked away, whistling.

Almost she called him back. But she managed to hold herself in check. Wretched Jarrod. How dare he be quite so care-free—and so very obvious about it— when he knew how miserable she was feeling. Not that she should be surprised, he was nothing but a smug, self-satisfied swine.

She was still fuming when she heard him get into the jeep. She couldn't see the jeep from where she was, didn't have to. Every sound at Marakizi had its own significance for her. There was nothing she did not know about the place. As she would one day know her environment in that very far-off city called Toronto, she reminded herself.

The jeep drove out of the gates. She saw it now. Jarrod was alone. No lion-hunting today. No need to worry about Jarrod today, said the small voice that she tried so hard not to hear.

In the end the loneliness and the inactivity got the better of her. The garden was looking neglected. The bougainvillaea near the guest-rooms needed cutting back. Armed with gardening-gloves and pruning-shears (all still where she had left them) she attacked the shrub with vigour. On the ground beside her, leaves and twigs began to pile up.

'Got rid of your frustrations?' asked an amused voice some time later.

She let her eyes rest on tanned legs bare to the thighs. From beneath long lashes she treated him to a look which revealed none of the longing which had sprung so suddenly to life inside her. Coolly she said, 'Some of them.'

'Every cut a symbolic jab into my own tender flesh.' He was laughing at her.

'How well you understand me,' she murmured.

He stood back, considering the shrub. 'I understand that you hate me—but did you have to brutalise this poor defenceless bougainvillaea?'

'Is it brutalised?' She gave a little sigh. 'Perhaps I did cut too much, but it will grow back.' She grinned suddenly, unable to resist him when he was in a light mood. 'You have an awful effect on me, Jarrod. You should have let me go, who knows what other havoc I might wreak on Marakizi.'

'I'll take my chances.' He reached out a hand and pushed a tendril of damp hair from her forehead, his fingers lingering a moment on the soft smooth skin at her temples. 'Whatever your feelings for me, I believe you still love this place.'

The touch unsettled her. Her breathing was uneven as she lifted her fingers to his and drew them away from her face.

There was intimacy in the moment. Such a strange kind of intimacy. Jarrod was in a creased safari-suit, with dust on his face and on his boots. Cathy, with her hair tied back in the kind of pony-tail she had not worn once in all her time in the city, was no less dirty. There was nothing loving between them—the simple caress was not an act of love. And yet there was a hint of the unquestioned intimacy that had once been between them.

'I think we both need a shower,' she said briskly.

'And then we'll have supper. You will join me for that I presume?' Jarrod cocked an eyebrow at her.

'I suppose I have no option.'

'None at all,' he agreed cheerfully. 'Don't look so stricken, Cathy. You have to eat, but you don't have to enjoy my company.'

'Do you care?' She could have bitten her tongue the moment the words were out. They were childish, and she didn't know why she'd said them.

Jarrod laughed again. 'That's irrelevant. We're getting divorced, remember?'

It was quite ridiculous that the words should strike such pain in her heart, but they did. Beneath the shower minutes later, Cathy tried to talk some sense into herself. I'm here to get Jarrod's consent. It's the one thing I want from him. The *only* thing ... And yet when he talks of divorce as if it's what *he* wants, I feel upset. Grow up, Cathy!

Together they braaied their meat, and watched the sun setting in the west. The crickets began their nightly shrilling, and from a distant kraal the rhythmic beating of drums echoed across the silent veld. Jarrod told Cathy about his work, and as before she listened absorbed. She wasn't being disloyal to Stewart, she told herself. It had been her work once too, it was only right that she should be interested.

Later, when it was quite dark, Jarrod brought out a packet of marshmallows and two long sharpened sticks.

'Not for me, thanks,' Cathy said carefully. Marshmallows brought back too many memories.

'The Cathy I remembered adored them.'

'Mushy things.'

'Right.' He was laughing at her again. It was a vibrant, earthy laugh, the kind of sound you could almost reach out and touch, Cathy thought, and she wished she could ignore the longing that was gnawing inside her.

She watched him warm a marshmallow for himself. Watched as he put it into his mouth and ate it.

She watched him pierce another marshmallow and hold it to the fire. 'I'll have one too,' she said then, temptation getting the better of will-power. As Jarrod had known it would, she knew, seeing the amused lift of his lips.

'Mushy,' she pronounced, a minute later.

'But perfect.'

'Perfect,' she agreed.

And she wondered with whom he'd been sharing marshmallows in the past year.

'I'm going out for the day tomorrow,' Jarrod said after a while. His voice was lazy, a little sleepy.

'Oh.'

'Like to come?'

'Thanks—but no.'

He turned his head to look at her. 'A girl of strong principles.'

He was mocking her, but in such a light-hearted way that she was uncertain how to parry his thrusts. 'Absolutely,' she countered lightly.

'Let me know if you change your mind.'

'I won't change it.'

'Well, that's fine too,' he said, and he sounded as if he meant it.

CHAPTER NINE

ALL night Cathy wrestled with her feelings. Jacob wrestling with the angel had nothing on her, she thought grimly. She wanted to go with Jarrod, but she knew that she wouldn't. Shouldn't. How she wanted to go with him! No, she would stay in the compound. The hours would pass.

She slept at length, but with sleep there came dreams. Dreams that brought a flush to her cheeks when she woke and remembered them.

The sun was beginning to rise when she went to the window and flung aside the curtains. The sky was still opaque, but Cathy, veteran observer of a bushveld sunrise, knew that it was going to be a perfect day. Hot—but perfect.

Jarrod would be out in the jeep, making his observation in the bush. He would stop somewhere and eat a picnic lunch in the jeep, and then he would drive again. Later he would return to camp, and he would file his notes for future analysis.

And what would Cathy be doing? Well, she had finished with the bougainvillaea, but there was a hibiscus that could do with some pruning. A frangipani that needed attention. And then ... She pushed a hand through her hair. She could always do some baking, yesterday's thoughts about the kitchen notwithstanding. A melktert, fresh from the oven, would taste good after supper tonight. Always supposing Jarrod had the right ingredients in stock.

It would be a quiet day, peaceful, tranquil. One of five peaceful tranquil days. So placid would she be by the time Stewart came to fetch her on Saturday that her fiancé would not recognise her.

'Ugh!' She did not know that she had said the exclamation of disgust out loud. She did know that she could not face spending today in camp, alone and tranquil.

Had Jarrod left? She ran to the door, pushed it open, and peered outside in sudden panic. It was just light enough for him to have left. From where she stood she could not see the spot where the jeep was parked. The compound was utterly quiet. There was not the whisper of sound, not the flicker of movement.

It took just a few seconds to pull jeans and a sweatshirt over her fragile nightgown. Then she ran to Jarrod's bungalow.

'Come in,' responded a voice to her knock at the door.

She pushed it open. 'Jarrod, I . . .' And stopped. He had come from the bathroom. A towel was slung around his neck, covering his chest, his hair was wet, and on his face was a smidgeon of shaving cream.

He grinned at her. 'Morning.'

She swallowed. 'Good morning.' It was hard to grin back at him. He was wearing shorts this morning, but his shoulders and chest, where the towel did not cover them, were as bare as the long taut legs. The very prototype of a virile male, the thought crossed her mind.

He stood watching her, his eyes quizzical, the faintest hint of a smile on his lips. He was waiting for her to speak.

'I changed my mind,' she said unsteadily, wishing her pulses would stop their pounding. She'd been married to the man for three years, for goodness sake, she knew every inch of him. Why was he affecting her in this most ridiculous way?

'A lady's prerogative. Changed your mind about what?'

'Don't tease,' she scolded, because if she'd spoken any other way there might have been emotions in her voice it was better for him not to hear. 'About coming with you today.'

'Good.'

Was that all? 'I was dressed and ready, and it seemed like a good day for a drive,' she said coolly.

The look of amusement in his face deepened, and she said, 'You've got shaving-cream on your face.'

'And your hair is tousled.'

She ran a confused hand through her hair. 'So it is. I suppose I forgot to comb it.'

'And the way you pounded on the door was so fierce it would have woken a baby.'

The expression in his eyes was making her feel weak at the knees. *Damn you, Stewart, you should have taken me with you. And damn you, Jarrod, for making me feel this way. I hate feeling this way.*

I also love it. God forgive me, I love it.

'All right,' she admitted. 'I was going back to do my hair. I thought you'd gone.'

'Come here,' he said softly.

Her alarm, as she took a step backwards, was intensified because she wanted so much to go to him. 'No.'

'Come here.' Could a whisper be a command?

'Don't be silly.' She looked at him a little wildly, wishing he wasn't quite so devastatingly sexy with that gleam in his eyes and the wicked look in his face. 'I have things to do,' she improvised. 'Hair to comb. A face to put on.'

'Your face looks terrific to me just as it is. And what's the point of combing your hair when I'm going to tousle it some more anyway?'

He came towards her, and she made no effort to escape. Her mind was saying one thing, her heart and her body another. She knew now that she'd made the choice at the moment when she'd knocked on his door.

The hands that pushed at him as he took her in his arms were little more than a token protest. He felt so *good*. His skin, where it touched her cheek, was cool and fresh, and his arms had just the right muscularity, and the slightly tangy scent of after-shave was a memory of the senses.

For at least half a minute they stood without moving, their bodies linked together only by the light circle of his arms. On the surface so casual. But a casualness that was belied by the frantic beating of their hearts, she could feel his heart right through her clothes.

She lifted her face a little, so that when she spoke her lips nuzzled the skin at the base of his neck. 'We shouldn't be doing this.'

'Why not?'

'It's not right.'

He looked down at her with a smile. 'Did you tell me when I married you that you were such an honourable lady? I doubt I'd have married you if you did.'

'I don't remember.'

'It really doesn't matter. We have a licence.'

'Soon to be cancelled.'

'Still in existence.' The smile was still in place, but his voice had grown husky. 'I'm your husband, Cathy.'

'We've been over all that,' she said desperately.

'So we have. I told you, my darling, that I would make love to you every time I felt like it. And that's what I intend doing.'

'It's not fair to Stewart.'

'Who's talking fairness? We're talking sex, and wanting, and desire.' He pulled her suddenly against him, so that she could feel every hard inch of his body. 'And you damn well know it.'

She knew that he wanted her. And that she wanted him.

'It was a mistake to come here.'

'A Freudian mistake then, if it was one at all. You wanted me to make love to you all the time.'

'I'm not going to answer that,' she said with an attempt at primness.

'You don't have to. I heard the answer in the fist that banged on my door, can see it in your eyes at this moment, can feel it in the heart that's thudding away through the sweat-shirt which I am going to remove.'

'Oh, stop talking so much,' she threw at him.

'A lady after my own heart.' He laughed softly. Then he said raggedly, 'As you've always been.'

His first kisses were sweet. Tender, playful, his tongue just brushing the outline of her lips. Loving, Cathy thought, and discarded the word as being inappropriate. Her eyes were closed, and she was letting him kiss her without responding, content to let him set the pace. She knew where it would end. Knew too that she could not resist him.

Forgive me, Stewart. Silently she sent the words across the miles that separated them. I can't seem to help myself but I'll make it up to you, I really will.

The kisses became deeper, hungrier, and at the same time his arms tightened, and his hands began to move along her back. There was no playfulness now, just a hunger and a need that communicated itself from one body to the other. Willingly Cathy responded to him now, her mouth parting, her hands moving to his neck above the towel, to bury themselves in his hair.

He broke the contact first. 'Were you always so tiny? I'm getting a crick in my back.'

She laughed up at him, the sound spontaneous and joyous on the silent air. 'Perhaps you've grown.'

'I stopped growing years ago. There is a way to kiss

you without having to bend.' Effortlessly he lifted her, so that her feet dangled five inches above the ground. It brought them even closer together, in a contact so erotic that she wondered how long she would be able to stand it.

'Nice,' he whispered.

'Mm,' she whispered back, her lips moving against his.

'We should have thought of it long ago.'

'Why didn't we?'

'Because we were stupid.' His voice roughened. 'In more ways than one.'

Her heart stopped quite still for a moment as she wondered what more he would say, and how she would respond. But he said nothing. He began to kiss her again, deeply, passionately, and she was kissing him back. He could not move his hands, but she could move hers, and she did, touching his face with its rugged cheek-bones, and then dropping them to his shoulders, to glory in the hard smooth feel of them, and then arching herself towards him so that she could reach the muscles that rippled in his back.

He let out a groan. 'And then there's another way,' he said.

'What's that?' she asked breathlessly.

'The best way.'

He did not put her down as he carried her to the bed. And she clung to him, sensation flooding through her at the movement of his legs against hers. None of her dreams had been quite like this.

Now we can both touch,' he said, as he put her on the bed, and then lay down beside her.

She touched his lips, tracing the outline with a finger. 'You're a bit of a rascal, you know.'

'I'd be more of a rascal if I stopped now.' Brown eyes held green ones, defying them to move away. 'Right?'

'Right,' she agreed huskily.

'Oh Cathy, Cathy, it's been so long. Too long!'
He groaned suddenly as he gathered her in his arms.

Her heart was beating wildly against her ribs, and her blood was singing. But in her head there was a voice that said, 'No word about love. Not a single word about love.'

He began to undress her. Up to this point he had held himself in control. A marvellous control for Cathy knew what depths of passion he possessed. He eased the jeans away from her legs and hips, and then it was the turn of the sweat-shirt. Now his hands held a touch of impatience, for the shirt was held fast against the sheet. Lifting herself slightly, Cathy helped him, as eager for there to be no barriers between them as he was.

'What on earth!' she heard him exclaim just as the shirt was going over her head. And then he laughed, a laugh of pure amusement.

'Jarrod?' She thrust the shirt from her head and stared at him.

'Oh, Cathy, darling Cathy.'

She followed his eyes, and saw the nightie she'd been wearing beneath her clothes.

'Oh dear . . .'

'A new style of dress?'

'I woke, and I thought you might have gone, and I just pulled on my clothes.'

'What a lovely sight. A memory, Cathy. I'll never forget it.'

'Neither will I.'

But there was a touch of sadness in her tone. A memory, that was all it would be. To add to the other memories. Which would be all that would remain of their marriage. As it should be, though Stewart might consider it a bit much. Not that she would ever tell him.

I shouldn't be so sad, she thought. I really shouldn't be so sad.

He drew the nightie over her head, and she pulled the towel away from his neck. For a long moment they lay quite still, as they remembered the feel of each other, the absolute rightness of the way their bodies seemed to fit together, all his hard bones and angles shaping themselves to her own soft curves.

And then they began to caress each other. His hands moulded themselves to her throat, moving downward till they were shaped over her breasts. Her eyes were closed again, and there was only sensation as he caressed her, first with his hands and his fingers, then with his lips. She did not need to open her eyes to caress him too. Every inch of him was as well-remembered as if they'd made love yesterday.

Their passion grew, intensified, and when the moment of fulfilment arrived it was the wild and wonderful thing it had always been. No greater joy than this, Cathy thought in a moment of pure exultation, and she said, 'Jarrod! Oh, Jarrod!'

For a long time they lay together, still entwined, not moving. Not wanting to move. As if afraid to break a spell.

At length Jarrod said, 'When was the last time we made love at dawn?'

'About thirteen months ago?' She hazarded the guess against his throat.

'Twelve months and one week.'

She shook with laughter, her fingers trailing lightly over his back. 'You kept a diary?'

'A mental one.'

'You really *are* a rascal.'

They laughed together, softly, their breath mingling, their bodies still clasped together.

'We'll have to get going soon,' he said after a while.

'Do we have to?'

He chuckled. 'You're wonderful. Prim one moment,

shameless the next. What am I to make of you, Cathy?'

'What do you think?'

'I'm only a poor confused male. Tell me.'

'Shameless at this moment.'

He ran his hand over her back and kissed her hair. 'I love you when you're like this.'

Only when I'm like this? But she didn't say it. She asked instead, 'Why do we have to go? And where?'

'To the lodges. Because I'm expected.'

'What a pity.'

He laughed again. 'We can always make a plan for later.' He drew away from her. 'Time to get up, wench.'

'If you say so.'

She lay back, hands behind her head, unconcerned at the picture she made. Caring only that she was with him. Not prepared to analyse the reasons why. Looking at him. Committing every inch of him to memory. The way his hair lay tousled after love, and the shape of his cheeks and his lips and his throat. His chest.

His chest!

She sat up with a cry. 'Jarrod! Your chest!'

His eyes, the wonderful eyes which had been warm and amused and passionate by turns this last hour, became suddenly narrowed and unreadable. 'Well?' He made no move to cover himself.

'Don't go cold on me! Please, don't go cold on me. Tell me what happened.'

He stood by the bed, a tall figure, well-built, muscular, face stern and remote. 'What do you want to know?'

'How it happened.'

She could not tear her eyes away from the terrible scars on his chest. Dark and vicious-looking. Not a straight scar. More like a welter of lines left by a vicious clawing.

'You were clawed!'

His face was a mask, detached, the face of a stranger. 'What of it?'

'What of it? I don't believe this! Why didn't you tell me?'

He shrugged, and she sat up straighter. 'I'm your wife, dammit.'

'Thanks for remembering.'

'Jarrod, you have to stop this. Talk to me.'

'Why do you only ask now?' He sounded bored.

'Because I didn't see it before.' She stopped, confused, wondering how that was possible. 'I really didn't,' she went on at last. 'Last night we were standing in the dark. And today ... Jarrod, you had a towel around you.'

'True.'

'I couldn't have seen. And afterwards, well we were lying so close together ...' She stopped, suddenly very angry. 'Why the hell am I talking so much? As though I have something to apologise for, when I haven't. What happened, Jarrod?'

The ghost of a smile cross his face. 'Persistent woman.'

'Believe it.' Slowly she said, 'The lion?'

After a moment he nodded.

'Oh Jarrod ... Jarrod, why didn't you tell me?'

'I must have forgotten.'

It wasn't important, said his voice. Something seemed to die inside her.

'It must have been terrible,' she said in a choked voice.

Jarrod made an impatient gesture. 'Can we talk about something else?'

'No! The same lion that's at large now?'

'Yes.'

'My God!' She remembered the apprehension which had been with her when she'd been out driving with Stewart. She'd known intuitively that Jarrod and Amos were out looking for the lion. 'My God, Jarrod, you could have been killed.'

'But I wasn't.'

Why was he doing this to her? 'When did it happen?'

His expression was shuttered. 'A while ago.'

'How long ago? Jarrod, this is like drawing blood from a stone.'

'I'd say it was more like an interrogation,' he countered coolly.

'You don't want my sympathy.' The words hurt to say them.

'Not now,' Jarrod said, and the meaning was not lost on her.

'I couldn't have known,' she whispered painfully.

'I suppose not.'

'Jarrod . . .'

She stopped. He was drawing a shirt over his head. He began to button it, and the scars were hidden. 'I have to go,' he said.

'Give me ten minutes.'

'You're still coming then?'

The look she gave him matched his own for coolness. 'Naturally. I don't change my mind that often. It's a long time since I saw the lodges. Might as well say my farewells before I leave Marakizi.'

Two could play the hurting game. She could wound just as he could.

He pulled on his trousers, his eyes resting briefly on the bare breasts which just minutes before had been warm beneath his lips. 'You may have half an hour. We've had nothing to eat.'

She didn't move until he had left the room. Even then she lay motionless. Her limbs were still heavy with the langour that comes after lovemaking, but the lovely feeling of wonder and beauty had gone. She became aware of her nakedness on the bed, and pulled the sheet over herself. A bit late for that now that Jarrod was no longer in the room, she thought wryly. All the same, there was a need for cover which had been missing before. It was only while there had been love that there had been no need for concealment.

Love! She sat up startled. But there had been no love. Hadn't it been sex all the time? Jarrod had said so, and she had agreed with him. Or had she?

Only now, when it was too late, did she acknowledge to herself that things were not as she'd made herself believe. Casual sex had never been her style. Nothing had changed in that respect. She could only make love with a man for whom she cared very deeply. It was why she had never been able to make love with Stewart. Why every moment with Jarrod had been sheer ecstasy.

And that raised new thoughts. What she had convinced herself was no more than intensely physical in nature had to be something else. True, the excitement, the vitality, the need that he aroused in her was sexual. But it was so much more besides. She loved him. She had always loved him, had never stopped loving him. She had tried to tell herself otherwise, and for a while she had succeeded in convincing herself of the fact. So much so that she had been prepared to make a new life with another man. And all the time the love had been there, suppressed, unacknowledged—but always there.

Which left her—where? With a man who desired her—oh, he desired her, of that there was no question—but only on a sexual level. A hurt and angry man, whose suffering lay deeper than she had ever realised. It was clearer now why he wanted her to stay at Marakizi a week. She'd guessed all along that he wanted to see her suffer, but she had thought it was only because she had left him. Now she knew that the lion had something to do with it. Jarrod must have thought she would come to him after the accident, unaware that she had not heard of it.

She would have come to him. Nothing would have stopped her. Not her own feelings of hurt and disillusionment, not her job in the city. She would have come, and she would have nursed him.

'I would have come if I'd known,' she said a while later, when she sat beside him in the jeep.

Dispassionate eyes turned her way, flicked her face briefly.

'I didn't know about the accident. I didn't know, Jarrod! I would have come.'

'Seeing the scars upset you?' It was a strange question.

'It tore my heart,' she said in anguish. 'Please tell me about it.'

He turned away from her, his eyes going back to the road. 'I'd rather not.' His tone was level, quite without emotion.

She sat in her seat, her body rigid with frustration. 'Jarrod . . .' She looked at him, but he did not respond. The rugged profile was remote and stern. His window was open and the breeze had blown his hair across his forehead. She longed to brush it back against his temples, to touch the hard-set lips and coax some softness into them. But she could not move. Less than an hour ago there was not an inch of her body those lips had not caressed and excited. She had felt free to touch and caress him in turn. Yet now she was unable to stretch out a finger to touch him. Unable only because she did not know what his reaction would be.

Tears filled her eyes, and she did not want him to see them. So she turned her head and pretended an interest in the scenery. So blurred were her eyes that an elephant could have crossed the road in front of them and she would not have seen it.

Beside her Jarrod had started to whistle, softly, almost under his breath. What was he thinking? Cathy did not believe that his show of uninterest was genuine. Men could make love when the whim took them, but there had been passion as well as tenderness in their lovemaking that morning. Was he thinking of that now? Would he make love to her again? Yes, she knew painfully, he would. But why? Why when there were other women available? He only had to go as far as the lodge to find several women who were crazy about him. And why with someone he despised?

She did not like the answer that came to her. Stewart had wanted there to be no ghosts left by the time she came to him. Jarrod's thoughts could be similar. Perhaps by making love to her he was laying ghosts of his own, was getting her out of his system. It was a painful thought.

If only he would talk about the lion. But it seemed that topic was taboo, and tense as she was, Cathy knew better than to bring it up again now.

She was glad that the tears had gone by the time they reached the first of the lodges. At least she would be able to present an air of cool composure.

There were two lodges, situated about twenty miles away from each other. Jarrod had worked very hard to make them what they were today. Beautiful places, they were famed not only in southern Africa but much further afield too.

As the jeep drove through the big stone gates of Flame Tree Lodge, Cathy thought it was no wonder that so many tourists came here from North America and from Europe. The big stone-walled building with its huge plate-glass windows stood where once there had been only bush. As they walked across the patio and through the lounge into the reception area, the tastefulness of the lodge made an impact on Cathy's senses. The lounge, decorated in a dramatic blending of blues and turquoise with splashes of bright yellow, was a beautiful room, bright and spacious. The walls were adorned with all manner of unusual African masks and the big windows gave on to a view of a water-hole just beyond the fence. Jarrod had chosen the site for this building carefully. At dusk tourists would sit in this room, or on the patio, looking out over the water, and watching the animals which came there to drink.

People returned to the lodges year after year. They were Jarrod's pride but he himself chose not to live there. Quiet, off-the-beaten-track Marakizi had always been his first choice of the place where he would lay his head at night. And until a year ago, when Marakizi had proved to be just too far away from civilisation, Cathy had felt the same way.

There was a new girl at the reception desk, and Cathy was glad. She had a few more minutes in which to compose herself before the inevitable meetings with people she knew. No more than minutes though. Word had spread quickly that she was here.

'Mrs Lundy, you're back!'

Cathy hugged Sara Barnes, the house-keeper, her smile hiding her shock at being called Mrs Lundy again after so long.

Sara was just the first of the staff who made a point of coming to talk to her. There were happy smiles, happy words, but there were also looks of curiosity. They must wonder where she had been all this time.

Sara insisted on taking Cathy on a tour of inspection. 'Everything looks wonderful,' Cathy said, and Sara beamed. She was a gem of a house-keeper, proud of every piece of polished wood, of the big windows that sparkled spotlessly in the morning sun.

Stopping to admire an arrangement of proteas mixed with long feathery grasses, Cathy said, 'This is beautiful. Do you still do your own arrangements?'

'Never let anyone else touch them.' Flower-arranging was Sara's passion in life. 'Let me know next time you come, Mrs Lundy, and I'll have an arrangement ready for you to take back to Marakizi with you.'

Jarrod had stopped beside them. Involuntarily Cathy glanced at him. Their eyes held a moment, and she wondered whether Sara's 'Mrs Lundy' had hit him as hard as it had hit her. The dark eyes were enigmatic, giving nothing away. She could not hold their gaze for more than a second.

Cathy turned back to the house-keeper. 'I've always admired your way with flowers, Sara, you've a real talent with them,' she said gently, and wondered what else she could have said.

After a light tea it was back to the jeep. As Jarrod took the road to Hibiscus House, Cathy said, 'Things seem to be going well.'

'Very well. We've had to close the waiting-list.'

'I see,' she said listlessly. And then, 'Will we see Helen?'

'Of course. She won't be as easy to fob off as Sara.'

'I don't suppose she will be,' Cathy responded tensely.

'I've always admired your way with flowers, Sara.' Jarrod's tone was mocking. 'Such quick-thinking, Cathy. A really smooth reply.'

Hating his sarcasm, she curled her fingers tightly into her hands. She'd hoped there would be a chance to try to talk to him again about the lion, but this was not the right time. In this mood Jarrod was a difficult man.

She did not want to ask the question, but something impelled her to voice it all the same. 'You've been seeing Helen, haven't you?'

'Haven't we talked along those lines once before?' He was still mocking her.

'I want to know.'

'So many things you want to know, Cathy.'

'I realise I have Stewart, but . . .'

'You ask too much,' he said roughly. 'You just ask too damn much.'

CHAPTER TEN

CATHY'S stomach was a tight knot by the time they approached Hibiscus House. This lodge was as lovely as the other, but she saw none of its beauty. Had she been a fool to come with Jarrod? she wondered. The day which had started so beautifully was rapidly becoming a nightmare. Pruning the shrubs at Marakizi might have been boring, but at least it would not have been traumatic.

Hibiscus Lodge was much like Flame Tree Lodge, except that the main building was surrounded by hibiscus, the trumpet-shaped flowers flashing scarlet and orange against the stone walls. It was already midday when Jarrod and Cathy arrived, and the wide shaded patio was filled with tourists, relaxing with cool drinks while they gazed into a vista of kopjies and river and bush.

Still beset by the feeling of depression that had been with her since they'd left Flame Tree Lodge, Cathy walked a little behind Jarrod as they went up the steps of the patio. Some of the staff were in the reception area, one face standing out from the others. Helen. Tall, lovely-figured Helen, with her dark hair hanging smoothly to her bare tanned shoulders, and a happy smile on her lips.

'Jarrod! I was hoping I'd see you.'

'Hello, Helen.' He was smiling too, his hand touching her cheek in a gesture of welcome. A very familiar gesture, Cathy thought painfully. The two knew each other well.

'I thought you might come.' Helen's face was upturned to his as she linked her hand through his arm. 'I have the sketches ready for you, and I . . .'

She broke off as her gaze alighted on Cathy. The light died in her eyes. 'Cathy ... I didn't know you were back.'

'I'd have thought the bush-telegraph would have carried the news long ago.' Forcing a smile she was far from feeling, Cathy kept her eyes averted from the hand on Jarrod's arm. 'I've been back at Marakizi a couple of days.'

'Nice to see you here,' Helen said, and Cathy knew she didn't think it nice at all. The girl had never made any secret of her feelings for Jarrod.

'It's nice to see you, too,' Cathy responded lightly. 'And nice to visit the lodge again.'

'I've a few things to do,' Jarrod broke in. 'Will you keep Cathy company, Helen? I'm sure she'd like to see the tiles you did for the dining-room.'

Reluctantly, it seemed to Cathy, Helen took her hand from Jarrod's arm. 'Would you like to see the tiles?' she asked, when Jarrod had walked away.

'Yes, I would.' Cathy's heart might be wrenching inside her, but she could put on an act—for a small while at least. 'Anything that concerns Hibiscus Lodge is of interest to me.'

'I wouldn't have thought so,' Helen said, a little sullenly.

Cathy was taken aback by the other girl's open rudeness. 'Both lodges are looking really good,' she said lightly, as they walked from one area to another. 'We've just come from Flame Tree, and Sara was showing me around there too.'

She heard Helen suck in her breath at that. Cathy did not like to hurt people, and she knew the remark had been hurtful, but Helen seemed to ask for it.

And then there was Jarrod. Cathy felt the need to defend herself, to fight. To fight for Jarrod? She didn't have to look far for the reason. She'd known it since that morning. If not since the moment she'd come back to Marakizi, she thought now, with a revelation born of hindsight. Helen did not have to know that the fight was probably futile, that Jarrod no longer loved his wife.

Unless he had told her so already.

The ceramic tiles on the dining-room walls were good. Very good. And Cathy told Helen so sincerely.

'I've been sketching for Jarrod,' Helen said, and there was something tight in her voice.

'I know. Thank you.'

'Why . . .' Helen looked startled. 'I suppose he's shown you the sketches?'

'He's mentioned them.'

'But has he shown them to you?'

'Not yet, but he will,' Cathy said easily. 'We've been busy with other things till now.'

And let Helen make of that what she wished.

The other girl was quiet a few moments. A number of emotions came and went in her face, none of them pleasant. Her hands were clenched at her side. At last she said, 'I've done some good work for Jarrod.'

'I've no doubt. You're an excellent artist. These tiles'—Cathy gestured—'they're really lovely.'

'We've been spending a lot of time together.'

So the girl was determined to make her statement. 'That's only natural in the circumstances,' Cathy responded lightly. Were it not for Helen's belligerence she would have some sympathy with the girl. Jarrod was an easy man to fall for, how well she knew it.

'Long time since you've been back.'

'Yes, it is.'

'Planning to stay this time?'

Cathy smiled, without answering. Had Helen thought herself well rid of Jarrod's wife? How much had he told her? Obviously not about the divorce, for Helen's surprise at seeing Cathy back had been genuine. Well, Helen would know the truth soon enough. Her suspense would last no more than a few days. Until then Cathy had no qualms at all about keeping her guessing.

I'm jealous, she thought when they were back in the jeep and driving to Marakizi. I'm jealous of Helen. Of the fact that she's been sketching for Jarrod, that she's been doing *my* work. And that's irrational because somebody has to do it.

But jealousy is irrational, and I never knew it before.

And I'm jealous of the time she's been spending with Jarrod. More jealous of that than of the sketching.

Firmly she kept her eyes on the bush. She saw the trees that had been broken by elephants, so that they lay on their sides, raw and splintered. She saw the vultures wheeling in the sky, and knew that somewhere in the long grass a kill had occurred, and that the birds were waiting for the predators to eat their fill, at which point they would swoop down for their share of the carcass.

She saw, and yet she did not see. For there was a part of her mind that could concentrate only on Jarrod. Jealousy was a painful emotion, she decided. Ugly, tearing at the insides of a person, just as the vultures would tear at the carcass. It was an emotion she had never experienced before. An emotion to which she had thought herself immune.

Now she knew how smug she had been. She had never had any reason to be jealous. So close had been her relationship with Jarrod that she had never suspected him of wanting to be with another woman.

She now knew something else too. Had it been Stewart with whom Helen had spent time, it would have meant little to her. Because I don't love Stewart, Cathy acknowledged with the painfulness of depair. And I do love Jarrod. I've always loved him. My foolishness was in thinking that I could stop loving him.

She turned her head to look at him, and he must have been aware of the movement because he turned too, and their eyes held.

'Enjoy the day?' he asked lightly.

'Very much,' she lied. 'It was wonderful to see the lodges again.'

'I'm glad.' There was a gleam in his eyes.

He knew that she'd hated the day, she thought grimly, and that satisfied him. Oh the arrogant man. He didn't deserve her love. How happy she would be if she could tear it from her heart and cast it to the wind that was blowing across the veld. But she could not. She was stuck with loving Jarrod. She'd go on loving Jarrod long after she was in Canada.

If she went to Canada. She sat up straight, startled at the thought. *If* she went to Canada . . .

Arriving back at Marakizi, Cathy found a message that Stewart had 'phoned, and that he would 'phone again. A pang of guilt stabbed her at thought of Stewart. In no way had she been fair to her fiancé. If only she could undo the events of this morning, the lovemaking when she had given herself body and soul to Jarrod. But it could not be undone.

And she knew that there was a part of her that exulted because it could not be undone.

In Jarrod's office she tried Stewart's number. There was no reply. She would try him again later, or he would 'phone her. Either way she would speak to him.

But there was something on Cathy's mind which worried her even more than Stewart. The lion. It had begun to obsess her. After supper that evening she tried again to speak to Jarrod about the animal which had been terrorizing the kraals, and which had left the awful scars on his body. As before, Jarrod refused to be drawn on the subject. Instead he began to talk of other things. Cathy wondered if he knew that despite the lightness in his tone, his lips had become a hard line and his jaw was tight.

That night she dreamed about the lion. A horrible dream. She woke out of it, sitting upright, screaming, and bathed in sweat.

Trembling, she lay back on the pillow and stared into the darkness, unable to shake off the terror of the dream. It was only a nightmare, she was able to tell herself. Yet the terror remained, as did the trembling.

She longed to go to Jarrod. To knock on his door, and crawl into the comfort of his bed. He would gather her into his arms, and he would hold her until the trembling had stopped. He would speak to her gently, and he would kiss her until all the horror was gone. There had been the odd nightmares in the past, and always Jarrod had been there for her.

She wanted to go to him so badly, and yet she could not. It was one of the many things she could not do. She loved Jarrod, loved him more than life itself. But there were things she could not do because he did not know that she loved him.

She could tell him ... She sat bolt upright in bed again, and wondered why the idea had been so long in coming. She would tell him so now. Sanity returned as she was pushing away the sheets. This was not the time for telling Jarrod anything.

Which brought her back to the lion.

In the end it was Amos who told her what she wanted to know. An Amos who had aged and become grey at the temples in the time Cathy had been away from Marakizi. She'd always thought he was ageless, this wonderful ranger who had been Jarrod's friend and right-hand man even before the lodges had begun to attract tourists. Now she realised that he was really quite old. Amos had grown up in the bushveld. He was a wiry man, alert to every sound and smell of the veld, conscious of the signals sent by the different animals, able to identify an animal by a fading hoof-print. Jarrod had always known how lucky he was to have Amos working with him.

He lived with his family in a kraal some little distance from the compound. He came to Marakizi the day after Cathy and Jarrod had been to the lodges. He wanted to see Jarrod. Cathy, who knew Jarrod was busy in the lab, took the chance to speak to the ranger herself first.

'Tell me about the lion,' she said without preamble. 'Please, Amos, I have to know.'

Much of the story Cathy knew already. The few bits of information she had elicited from Jarrod had been enough to piece together a picture of an errant lion which had taken to making a nuisance of itself. That the lion was elusive she had realised too, but her first inkling that the trouble had been going on for quite some time had come when she'd seen Jarrod's scars. Scars that were vivid but not so raw as to be new.

The old man's face was grave as he told the story, the words coming out slowly. He told of the hunt, of how he had gone with Jarrod to shoot the lion. But the lion had ambushed them, and both men had been hurt.

'When did it happen?' Cathy asked.

Amos hesitated, then grew silent. He looked at Cathy, then looked away, his face troubled.

'When?' she persisted, though with a shivering certainty she thought she knew already. 'Many months ago, Amos? When the baby was supposed to be born?'

The old man nodded, without meeting her eyes. He was uneasy because he had broken the conspiracy of silence he shared with Jarrod, Cathy knew. Men, she thought on a wave of anger and despair. For reasons only known to themselves, they had decided not to tell her the truth about that dreadful day when they had nearly lost their lives, and Cathy had lost the baby.

Of course she understood now why Jarrod had told her nothing about the lion at the time. He had not wanted her to worry. But what had kept him from contacting her and telling her the truth later? There had been time enough for him to do that, she'd been in the flat two months before she'd decided to move. He could have written, could have 'phoned from the lodges. What had kept him from telling her the story on her return to Marakizi? How well she remembered the first evening at the camp-fire. Amos had come to talk to Jarrod about the lion, and then she'd questioned Jarrod and he had refused to talk, had turned the conversation away to other, more frivolous matters.

Above all, why hadn't he told her yesterday, when they had made love and she had seen the scars for the first time?

It could only mean one thing. He felt that she had let him down when he'd needed her, and now he no longer wanted her in his life. The situation was ironic.

'Why has it taken so long to find the lion?' she asked.

Amos lifted his shoulders. There were lions with the deviousness and the cunning of the devil himself, and this lion was one of them. 'It's been making trouble all this time?'

'No.' He shook his head. It had been lying low. For months there had been no sign of it, so that they had thought it had gone elsewhere, to the Kruger National Park perhaps, or to one of the other private game parks. And then it had reappeared.

'The other day, was that the first time you'd been after it since the accident?' That would be too hard to believe. 'Surely not?'

No, there had been other times. But always the lion had eluded them.

'You'll go again?'

The old ranger met her eyes. 'It is necessary.'

Yes, it was necessary. Much as Cathy loathed the idea of Jarrod and Amos endangering their lives, she knew it was necessary that this one lion be killed.

'Thank you for telling me,' she said at length. Gently she added, 'Please, don't tell Jarrod that I know.'

Amos lifted his head. The look he gave her was wary, but it was not puzzled. It was as if he understood why she did not want Jarrod to know. She wished she understood the reason fully herself.

Oh, it was all there, in a vague sort of way. Jarrod did not want her to know. He would not take kindly to the fact that she had wormed the story out of Amos. But there was more to it than that, Cathy thought, as the old ranger walked away in the direction of the laboratory. Much more.

Almost of themselves, her feet took the path to the fence, stopping when they got to the spot where her elbows had worn the indentations in the top of the wood. She leaned her arms on the wood and looked out across the bush, where an eland, regal and lovely, was making its way towards the river. How she loved this place, she thought, her eyes blurring with tears so that the eland was no longer visible. Marakizi, the bush and the compound and the animals, they were a part of her. As Jarrod was a part of her.

She was a one-man woman. How could she ever have believed otherwise?

Which took her where? A blunt confrontation with Jarrod? It would yield nothing. She could tell him what she knew, and they could talk about it. But the exercise would be futile. Jarrod would have to know that she'd learned what had happened, but she could not confront him with it. If there was to be any hope of a future with him—dare she even let herself dream about a future at this late stage?—then she must find the right time for the telling. And who knew when that would be?

Stewart 'phoned again that night. 'Your beloved is on the line for you,' Jarrod said lightly when he came to call her, and Cathy just smiled and said, 'Thank you, I'll go and talk to him.'

Her hand was shaking as she picked up the receiver and said, 'Hello, Stewart.'

'How are you, Cathy love?'

'My nose is burnt and my cheeks are full of freckles.'

'And your fingers are stiff from sketching giraffe.'

After a moment she said, 'What makes you say that?'

'I have a vivid imagination.'

And what else have you guessed? Oh God, Stewart this is going to be hard.

'And how are you?' she asked, after a pause that had lasted just seconds too long.

'Fine. It's been a busy few days. But I'm looking forward to seeing you on Saturday.'

'About Saturday . . .' She stopped. Her throat was dry, and the hand on the 'phone was white-knuckled.

'Cathy?'

'It would be better'—she closed her eyes—'if you didn't come.'

There was a long silence. Then Stewart said, 'I see.'

'No, you don't,' she said a little desperately.

'I think I do.' She could not quite define the note in his voice. 'You and Jarrod have got back together.'

'No.'

'Tell me,' he said, after a moment. 'You know you can.'

And suddenly she knew that she could tell him. 'I love Jarrod.' She said it simply. All day she'd been wondering how she was going to break it to Stewart, words and phrases had whirled in her mind, and in the end she just said it simply.

After what seemed a long silence, Stewart said, 'I think I understand.'

'Just like that?' She was incredulous, and her throat felt thick. 'I don't know what to say. I didn't expect this to be so easy. I mean, I thought I'd have to convince you.'

He gave a short laugh. 'There must have been a part of me that understood all along.'

'I don't know what to say,' she said again, shakily.

'The moment I set eyes on that husband of yours I knew why you'd been holding back with me. Because you were holding back, you know.'

'I never realised the reason,' she whispered.

'Didn't you?'

'You're being so understanding,' she said at last.

'I don't feel the slightest bit understanding. Part of me curses the day we came to Marakizi.'

'Stewart . . .'

His voice changed as he went on, and it was as if he had not heard her cut in. 'But it was probably the right thing to do.'

'Why, Stewart, why?' She had to know why he felt the way he did.

'I told you that I didn't want you bringing any ghosts into our marriage.'

'You did.'

'Jarrod would have been a tough ghost for me to kill.'

'Yes.' She laughed shakily. 'I'd like to say otherwise, but it wouldn't be true.'

'God, Cathy, have I been a crazy fool?' Stewart asked with sudden passion. 'You offered to be my mistress. Why the hell didn't I take you up on it?'

'You know why.'

'We could have had such a darned good life together. I'd have been good to you.'

She dashed a hand to her eyes. 'I know.'

'Are you crying?' he asked.

'Yes, you should see what I look like. Dusty tears over freckles, a real mess. Stewart, I know I'd have been happy in Canada. But I love Marakizi, it's where I belong. And I love Jarrod.'

'So you've forgiven him for not being there when you needed him?'

'There's nothing to forgive. He couldn't have come. He'd gone after a lion. That same lion, do you remember it? And he was mauled.'

On a new note, Stewart said, 'And now the two of you have made things up and intend to live happily ever after.'

'Nothing like that.'

'You've lost me.' He sounded really surprised now.

'He doesn't want me.'

'The bloody fool. Come with me, Cathy.'

'That wouldn't be fair to either of us.'

After a moment Stewart said, 'I suppose I was just casting a straw to the wind. Have you told him how you feel?'

'Not yet.'

'Then . . . what are you going to do?'

'I haven't decided.'

'Fight for him,' Stewart said with sudden vehemence. 'It's what I should have done with you, and I don't believe I'm saying this—but if you really love him, then fight to keep him.'

'You're the best man that ever walked this earth, do you know that?' Cathy's voice was choked.

'You're convincing me.'

'Stewart—be happy. You'll find someone else. There's Anna—she loves you I think. You deserve something better than I would have been.'

'Be happy too,' he said very softly.

She was about to say something more, but he had

put down the receiver. And after a moment Cathy was glad. There was nothing more either of them could have said.

Cathy did not tell Jarrod that Stewart was not going to be coming for her. He might have been curious about the call, but he asked no questions, and she volunteered no information.

And by Friday there were other things on his mind.

The lion had been seen near the kraals again. Jarrod was going with Amos the next day to hunt it down. This time, he said when pressed, they were going to get it.

'Take me with you,' Cathy said.

'Not a chance.'

'Please.'

'No.' His voice was hard. 'That's my last word on the matter.'

Just before sunset on Friday Amos send word that he was ill. One of his grandsons came from the kraal with the message. Jarrod sent word back that Amos was not to worry.

'You'll wait for another opportunity?' Cathy asked.

She saw him hesitate. 'Perhaps,' he said after a moment.

'You're lying. You're going after the lion, I know.'

'I don't want to talk about it.'

'I do.'

'Leave it alone,' he said irritably.

'I'm your wife Jarrod.'

'Temporarily only, I believe.'

She bit her lip. 'Jarrod, please . . .'

'No, Cathy. And that's final.'

Final where Jarrod was concerned perhaps. Not final for Cathy. Jarrod must have forgotten that once she'd made up her mind she was a woman to be reckoned with. Perhaps she had forgotten herself until now. She was going with him tomorrow, though she would keep her silence for the moment because there was no sense in antagonising him further.

It was not the only issue on which she was keeping silent, she reflected wryly.

CHAPTER ELEVEN

THEY had their nightly braaivleis under the stars. It was a silent meal. Cathy tried to make conversation but Jarrod did not respond. At length Cathy fell silent too. She sat in the dark, listening to the shrilling of the crickets and the barking of distant baboons, and in the flickering light of the kerosene lamp she watched her husband. The brooding face had never looked more rugged than tonight.

She wanted to reach out to him, not only physically but mentally too. To give him some comfort and love and to lessen the worry that weighed on his mind. She knew that he was thinking of the next day, of the lion, and she wished that he would talk about it. She also knew that he wouldn't.

Unlike other evenings, Jarrod didn't put a fresh log on the fire when the meal was over. Cathy watched him throw water over the grey coals, and saw that his shoulders were bunched rigid.

'Time to turn in,' he said.

'All right.'

'I'll walk you to your room.'

'Thanks.'

At the door of the cheetah-room he said a brief good night. It was on the tip of Cathy's tongue to say, 'Will I see you before you go off tomorrow?' But she knew what his answer would be. 'Sure,' he'd say, and he'd be lying through his teeth. By the time she awoke he would be gone. And so she stayed silent as he walked away in the darkness.

The room, hot from the sun that had burned on the walls and roof the whole day, seemed emptier than ever. Somehow unable to shower and get ready for bed, Cathy paced up and down. Six steps one way, six the other. The picture on the wall opposite the bed drew her eyes, and she stopped pacing to look at it. A simple arrangement of flowers. But what memories it held.

A breath shuddered through her. Swiftly she began to shed her clothes, and slid a silk night-gown over her head, smoothing it over her breasts and shoulders. In a drawer was a bottle of perfume she had not used since coming to Marakizi. Uncorking it, she applied a few drops to her wrists and ears and to the hollow between her breasts.

Then she went to the mirror and took a long look at herself. The nightie clung seductively to her slender figure. In the soft light her eyes were long-lashed and mysterious, and her hair was slightly ruffled, as if a breeze had played through it with gentle fingers.

Cathy the seductress, she thought in wry amusement. I've never played the role before.

She left the cheetah-room and made for Jarrod's bungalow. A light was shining through the curtained window. So he had not been able to sleep either. Lightly she tapped on the door.

'Come in,' he called, and she went inside.

'Something wrong, Cathy?' And then, on a new note, 'Why Cathy!'

She went up to the bed. He'd been lying back against the pillows, but now he sat up.

'Cathy?' he said again, and she saw his eyes move slowly over her figure in the almost transparent garment.

'I couldn't sleep,' she said softly.

'Tried counting sheep?' he asked lightly.

'I know something better.'

'You could try saying the alphabet backwards.'

From beneath her lashes she gave him a look. 'Do you really want me to go back to my room?'

There was tension in the lines around his mouth, but in his eyes was a smile. 'This is a new side of the girl who's always waited to be invited.'

'People change.'

She tugged at his blanket, and slid underneath it.

'You know how to choose your times, don't you?' he said ruefully, as he shifted to make room for her.

She pretended not to know what he was talking about. 'Oh, I think so.' Turning, she nestled against him. 'I think I could sleep very well here.'

He laughed, but his voice was husky. 'Witch.'

He was pleased she'd come, she could sense it. But he was not responding as she'd hoped. Jarrod was such a physical man, so easily stirred. For him to be passive now must mean that his anxiety was even greater than she'd realised.

She moved against him, her lips trailing over his chest and into the hollow at the base of his throat. His body stiffened as she melted against him, her arm sliding beneath his neck, drawing his head towards hers. Always it had been Jarrod who had aroused her, who had played the role of the seducer, teasing her, tantalising her, until she lost her sanity and her control. This time it was Cathy. She was making love to him, sheer female instinct driving her, telling her what to do.

At length he gathered her to him with a groan. 'Are you trying to drive me out of my mind?'

'Yes!' She was unashamed. 'Love me, Jarrod. Please love me.'

His lips moved against hers. 'Not tonight.' He kissed her, but there was no passion, just a weary tenderness. 'Not tonight, Cathy.'

As far as Jarrod knew there would be no tomorrow. Could he have forgotten that tomorrow was Saturday, and that Stewart was supposed to be coming? Cathy did not intend to remind him of the fact.

'All right,' she said gently. 'But I want to stay with you all the same.'

'Yes,' he said. 'I'd like that.'

He kept his arms around her, they were still around her when he fell asleep. Cathy lay awake, listening to the breathing that had become slow and steady, loving the feel of the long body that touched hers from the tips of her toes to the top of her hair, enjoying the smell of him in her nostrils. Desire stirred inside her, filling her body with an aching need. She'd wanted to make love with him. She still wanted it. But there was some consolation in lying with him, in being able to love him while he slept.

She must have been crazy even to think she could stop loving him. Right from the moment she'd set eyes on him a week ago, she'd known that the flame that had always sparked between them was as strong as ever. But in those first days she'd tried to convince herself that the flame was no more than physical attraction. And then she'd discovered that she still loved him despite all that she had thought had happened. The months apart had changed nothing. If anything, she loved him even more than before.

Very gently, so as not to wake him, she disengaged herself from his arms and left the bed. He did not stir as she moved silently around the room. She came back to the bed, and as she lay down he grunted in his sleep, reached for her, and held her to him.

It was early dawn when Cathy awoke. Jarrod was no longer in bed with her. He was walking around the room, opening drawers and closing them, picking up clothes only to drop them again. A frustrated man.

'Good morning,' Cathy said after watching him a few moments.

He looked her way. 'Morning.'

'Going out to hunt the lion?'

'When I find the keys of the jeep. Hell, Cathy, I could swear I put them in the usual place in the drawer.'

'Are you going to take me with you?'

'We've already been over that,' he said irritably. 'You know the answer.'

'You'll take me,' she said softly.

'Give me one good reason.'

There was a jangling sound as she said, 'This reason.'

He looked startled. And then he advanced on her. 'Give me those keys.'

She hid them beneath her. 'When you agree to take me with you.'

'No, Cathy, no.'

'Then the keys will stay where they are.'

'I could force them from you.' There was a note of danger in his tone.

She met his eyes, steady and unafraid. 'But we both know you're not a violent man.'

He came to the bed and stood looking down at her, tall and sleek in a crisp safari-suit. He touched her face, then moved down to the slender curve of her throat. 'Mata Hari had nothing on you,' he said in a tone that was a mixture of amusement and exasperation.

She looked back at him, her heart beating fast in her chest. She pulled a little away from him, and as she did so the blanket fell away from her, and she tugged it back up.

Jarrod let out a shout of laughter. 'Last night you were all seduction, and this morning you go coy on me. Stewart won't know how to handle you.'

'Are you going to take me with you?' Didn't he know that she hadn't gone coy on him? That the reason she'd pulled on the blanket was to keep the keys concealed.

Jarrod shoved an impatient hand through his hair. For a moment he stood looking at her, a sardonic glitter in his eyes. 'Men are such fools,' he said at last. 'That sexy scene last night, I believed you were after my body, and all the time it was just a ploy. You waited till I was asleep and then you stole the keys.'

It wasn't only the keys, she wanted to say. If I didn't love you so much I wouldn't have slept in your bed. But she met his gaze and said, 'Of course.'

He tugged the blanket away from her, and pulled her out of the bed and against him. 'You don't know what you're letting yourself in for. Going after a truant lion is one hell of a dangerous business.'

'Do you think I don't know that?'

'Then stay here.'

'No. I'm not a faint-hearted girl, Jarrod, you should know that. I want to be there.'

'So that you can see all the action?' he demanded roughly. 'Is that it, Cathy? So that you can regale all those Canadians with tales of a lion-hunt in the African bush? What a topic for dinner conversation.'

Later she could tell him that there would be no Canadian dinner-conversations. Not now.

'I don't want you to go alone,' she said simply.

He made a sound in his throat, she was so close to him that she felt it rather than heard it. She was so close to him that the familiar excitement was beginning to build up inside her. She kept very still. This was not the time to inflame him. There was a lion to hunt, before it could do more harm.

'I'm coming with you,' she said, 'whether you agree or not.'

For a moment his hands tightened convulsively on her back. Then he said, 'All right, I can't go on fighting you. But you'll listen to what I say. Obey every order. Promise, Cathy?'

She nodded. And they both knew that it was a promise she might break if she thought it necessary.

An atmosphere of tranquillity hung over the awakening bushveld. The air rang with bird-song. Here and there herds of impala grazed, and in a clearing were two giraffe. Cathy did not bother to ask Jarrod if they were ones with transmitters. There were other things on both their minds.

For the tranquillity was deceptive. In the bush somewhere was a dangerous lion.

'You hate to shoot an animal,' Cathy said, looking at her husband's tense face.

'I loathe it. But there are times when it has to be done. The lion has tasted human blood. The hunting-scene has changed for this particular animal. It will attack again. And this time it might kill someone.'

'Do you know where to look?'

'There's a donga . . . We thinks it hangs out there.'

'You saw the lion the last time you went after it?'

'We saw the spoor. Amos was certain it was the correct spoor.'

Jarrod's voice was quiet. He was a man who kept his head even when a situation became dangerous. But Cathy saw that the hands that held the wheel of the jeep were white-knuckled. Inside him the tension was great.

She did not question whether Amos could have been wrong about the spoor they'd seen. The old ranger did not make mistakes of that kind.

They had been on the road about an hour when Jarrod stopped the jeep. Cathy threw him a questioning look, 'This is it?'

'This is it,' he echoed her briefly. 'The donga is half a mile or so from the road.'

'You're not taking the jeep any further?'

'It's woody terrain. We'd never make it.'

'Quite a spot.' Now that the moment had come, Cathy experienced a fear that she would not admit to Jarrod.

'Quite a spot,' he agreed. 'You'll stay in the jeep.'

'I'm coming with you.'

'You agreed to obey orders.'

'I'm coming with you, Jarrod. You know that I'm coming.'

Beneath his tan his face was pale. But the eyes that met hers were steady. Without a word he reached for his gun, and then gave another one to her.

'You knew I'd come,' she said.

'I know you're a stubborn woman.' There was just the very faintest hint of a smile in the dark eyes. 'You'll need this, Cathy. But fire only if I say so. Don't let panic make you trigger-happy.'

'I promise,' she said, and this time she meant it. There were situations that called for the utmost discipline. This was one of them.

They left the jeep and went into the bush. Jarrod taking the lead, they began to walk. Silently, carefully. Cathy felt the sweat of fear pricking her skin. In the compound at Marakizi, or at the lodges, she was never frightened. Predators could be a hundred yards away, but there was always a fence between the animals and the humans. Walking through the veld, not knowing what could be in the long grass or behind a bush, was a different experience altogether. Very frightening.

Somewhere, perhaps not far away, there was a lion with a taste for human blood. Cathy's grip tightened on the gun. She wished it didn't feel as ineffectual as a walking-stick.

Now and then Jarrod stopped, and Cathy, a few paces behind him, stopped too. No words passed between them, none were necessary. He was scouting the bush. Listening, searching. Alert to every movement, every whisper in the long dry grass. If the lion had walked this way it was hard to detect its spoor, for there was only underbrush here.

If only Amos, with his special instinct for the bush, was with them. There were things he would be able to tell from the bend of the grass or the sound of a bird. But his absence did not make Cathy regret that she'd come. However frightened she was, to have remained at Marakizi would have been infinitely worse. There would have been the knowledge that Jarrod was alone and in danger. There would have been the waiting.

They came to the donga. It was a big swampy area. There was mud underfoot now, on it the marks and footprints of animals. Jarrod paused, half-turned, and gestured. Cathy saw a lion's spoor.

They were close.

At the side of Cathy's neck a nerve began to throb. The hand that gripped the gun was wet. Jarrod's gun was held at the ready. His shoulders were taut, his throat corded.

The lion came upon them suddenly, charging at them from behind its ambush of rocks. Jarrod let out an exclamation. The gun sounded. And then the wounded lion rolled against Jarrod, throwing him off balance, pinning him to the ground.

Later the scene would return to Cathy in the form of recurrent nightmares. But now there was no moment of panic. No moment for thought. In seconds she had lifted the gun and pointed it at the lion's head.

A second shot rang out, echoed across the veld. The silence that followed was infused with a kind of after-roar. And then some birds set up a wild squawking.

Cathy heard none of it. For a long moment she stood frozen, quite unable to move, looking at the fallen animal and the man pinned beneath it.

The lion was dead.

What of Jarrod? Oh God in heaven, what of Jarrod? She watched in disbelief as the lion seemed to roll away from the man, to lie obscenely on the ground. Then she ran to Jarrod. His eyes were closed, and his face was white, and he was not moving.

'Oh God,' she sobbed aloud, 'Let him be alive. Please let him be alive.'

'I'm alive.' The words emerged faintly from bloodless lips, and the dark eyes fluttered open.

She dropped beside him. 'Jarrod! Oh, Jarrod, thank God!'

'And you. I think you just saved my life.'

'I did what I had to.'

His lips twisted in a painful grin. 'This is a heck of a place for a chat. I seem to have hurt my arm. Help me up, Cathy, we have to get out of here.'

As gently as she could she helped him to his feet. His arm was hurting him badly, and his face was still very pale.

She carried his gun as well as her own, and they made it back to the jeep without incident. Cathy drove back to camp, glancing aside now and then to see how Jarrod was taking the journey. She was relieved when she saw that a little of his colour had returned.

'I never could stand a woman who says "I told you so",' he teased once when their eyes met.

'Must have been a moment of weakness when you said I had saved your life.' What a relief it was that they were able to tease.

'No,' he said simply. 'I meant it.'

For a long moment their gaze held, and then Cathy turned her eyes back to the road, glad of the excuse to hide her emotions. Didn't Jarrod know that she really would give her life for him? That without him there was no life for her?

Didn't he know by now how much she loved him? And if he did not know, would she have the chance to convince him?

After a while he said, 'You've been remarkable.'

'Thank you.' This time she did not look at him.

'Quick straight aim, and that from someone who hates to shoot. No panic.'

'There was no time for panic,' she said truthfully.

'You're a gutsy woman, my darling.'

'Thanks.' She swallowed hard. 'You're a gutsy man, Jarrod.'

As with many tense situations, reaction only set in a while after the danger was past. For Cathy it happened when she had accompanied Jarrod to his room, and had helped him into bed.

She looked at him, lying back against the pillows, and her body was seized by an awful trembling.

'Come here,' he said, his voice concerned, his good arm curved in invitation.

She went to him, willingly, seeking his warmth and his reassurance. She lay down beside him on the bed. Then she began to weep.

His hand moved gently on her hair. 'My brave girl,' he said when the weeping had stopped.

She turned her head to look at him. 'I was so frightened.'

'You were magnificent.'

'I thought you'd be killed.'

There was a strange expression in his eyes. 'Didn't you have any thought for yourself?'

She was uncertain all at once.

'Shift over a little,' he said roughly. 'I want to kiss you.'

She lifted herself higher against the pillows, positioning herself so that they could kiss. While she had been weeping his closeness had provided a blessed comfort. Now, with the reaction over, excitement began to fill her body. She yearned for his passion, but she was careful how she lay against him, aware of his sore arm, not wanting to hurt him more.

'This isn't good enough.' He moved, wanting to

gather her against him. And then she heard his gasp of
pain.

'Easy,' she whispered. His right arm had been badly
bruised when the lion had fallen on him. The bruises
would take a few days to heal.

He lay still a few moments. Suddenly he laughed.

'What's the joke, Jarrod?'

'I'm just thinking of the irony of the situation.
Last night I could have made love to you, and I
didn't. And now I want to make love to you, and I
can't.'

'But I can,' she said softly.

'Cathy?'

'Let me show you.'

'I can't even take my clothes off.'

'I can,' she said.

With infinite gentleness she began to do just that.
Careful not to hurt him more than she had to, she
eased the shirt from his back, then proceeded to
remove the rest of his clothes.

'You have the advantage over me,' he said huskily,
when she'd finished.

'Not for long.'

As she undressed herself she was aware of his
quickened breathing, of his eyes on her body. She was
aware of her own desire and need.

Lying down beside him once more she began to kiss
him. It was as if their roles had been reversed. She was
the one who led, who set the pace, brushing a trail
around his mouth and his eyes, and then down to his
throat.

Every movement of his right arm and shoulder hurt
him, rendering the long hard body almost immobile,
but he managed to cup the back of her head with his
left hand, guiding her, so that her mouth went back to
his. They kissed, a long deep kiss, and she heard him
groan in his throat.

'Make love to me,' he pleaded. 'Make love to me, Cathy.'

Always in the past Jarrod had been the dominant one. This time it was Cathy. Drawing on all the love and need that was in her, all the fierce female instinct, she made love to him. And Jarrod let her do as she wished. She caressed him with her lips and her hands, arousing a hunger both in him and herself. Hands and mouth roamed at will over the scarred chest, around his navel, his hips, and back to his face.

'Lovely,' he groaned. 'Lovely.' And then at length, 'Cathy darling, let me love you too.'

She lifted herself higher in the bed, so that he could reach her breasts. With his good hand he began to caress her, and she closed her eyes against the tormenting worship that was in his face and his fingers. Deep inside her a fire raged and the words shouted in her mind, I love you, Jarrod. Oh, I love you.

They had made love often in the past, but there had never been a time like this one. The passion, the excitement were there in abundance, but there was also a great tenderness. It was even stronger than the passion, overwhelming and engulfing them both, so that they called out each other's names in a kind of frenzy.

Afterwards Cathy lay against Jarrod while he stroked her gently, glorying in the soft caresses, keeping her head turned so that she could rest her lips against his chest.

'That was marvellous,' Jarrod said at length.

Cathy sat up so that she could look at him. 'I thought so too.'

'No false modesty in you,' he teased.

The expression in his eyes made her heart beat fast once more. 'Not when it's uncalled for.'

'Come back here,' he growled. 'I like it when your mouth nuzzles me . . . Ah yes, like that!'

They lay together a long while, bodies entwined, hearts beating as one, limbs languorous. She could lie like this forever, Cathy thought, and never grow bored with it.

And then Jarrod said, 'What day is it?'

'Saturday.'

'Oh lord, your wretched fiancé will be here any time, had you thought of that? What on earth will you tell him?'

Softly Cathy said, 'Stewart's not coming.'

'Why not?' Jarrod sounded surprised.

'I told him not to.'

'*You* told him . . .' And after a moment, 'Why?'

'You want to know a lot, don't you?'

'Yes, damn you, woman, I do.'

He pushed himself up, forgetting, only to fall back on a wave of pain. Cathy saw the pallor of his face, and the beads of sweat on his forehead, and her heart went out to him. Oblivious of her nakedness, she left the bed and fetched a hand-towel, and came back to him and wiped his face.

'You must rest,' she said gently.

'How the hell do you expect me to rest when questions are churning inside me?'

'Ask them then.'

'Why did you insist on coming with me today? You must have known there'd be danger.'

The change of topic surprised her, but she did not comment on it. She merely said, 'That's why— because it was dangerous.'

'That's no reason.'

'I didn't want you to be alone.'

'But why, Cathy, why?' Urgency throbbed in his voice.

'Because I love you,' she said simply.

There! It was out. A great relief settled over her. She had said the words. No matter how Jarrod felt or reacted, she'd said what she'd been wanting to say for days. Whatever happened now, she would never regret having told him.

He looked stunned. 'Say that again.'

'I love you.'

'I don't believe this.' Jarrod, her strong self-sufficient Jarrod, looked dazed. At last he asked, 'Why did you tell Stewart not to come today?'

'Same reason. Because I love you.'

'As much as I love you?' He groaned suddenly. 'As much as that, Cathy my darling?'

'I didn't think you did ... still do ...' She was shaken by the violence of his feelings.

'My God, Cathy, what do you think this long week's been all about? Do you think I'd have bothered to put us both through this ordeal if I didn't love you so much?'

She could only look at him through a blur of happiness, as she tried to assimilate what he'd said. For the first time she understood, at least she understood some of it. She wanted him to elaborate, but he said, 'Kiss me, darling. Bring your face here and kiss me.'

Afterwards, a long while afterwards, they were able to talk again.

'Is Stewart coming another day?' Jarrod asked.

'He's not coming at all.'

There was a silence before the next question. 'What did you tell him?'

'That I loved you.'

Jarrod looked at her disbelievingly. 'You told him that before he left here?'

'I told him on the 'phone. The day we came back from the lodges.'

'Why the hell didn't you tell me?'

'I didn't think you were ready to hear it.' It was so easy to talk now. 'I didn't know if you wanted to hear it.'

'If I wanted . . . How could I not want it? You're in my blood, Cathy. In my heart, my dearest darling love.'

'And you're in mine. Oh, Jarrod . . .'

They clung together in a kiss that had no meaning in time.

Presently Jarrod said, 'How did Stewart take it?'

'With a good deal of grace. I think he expected it.'

'I wanted to kill him, do you know that?'

'You'd have done away with a fine man.' She swallowed on the lump in her throat. 'He's a good man, Jarrod, and I hurt him badly.'

'He knew you were married.'

'He thought the marriage was over. Jarrod, you have to know, that night, after you insisted I stay here, I went to Stewart and said I'd live with him without being married.'

She looked at Jarrod's murderous expression, and away from it, and hoped she had not destroyed everything with her words. 'I still hoped I could fight my feelings for you. Stewart . . . Stewart told me to stay here, to make sure you weren't what I wanted. I think he knew the truth by then.' She was silent a few moments, remembering the last morning with Stewart, and the 'phone call. 'And then, on the 'phone . . . He told me to fight for you.'

'Well I never.' Jarrod looked amazed.

'There are some noble men in this world, my darling, even though you don't happen to be one of them.'

'You'll pay for that.' He reached out a finger and traced an erotic path around the shape of one breast. 'What else did you tell this noble man?'

'About the lion,' Cathy said.

The finger stopped its path abruptly. Jarrod grew very still. 'What about the lion?'

'I told him that you'd gone after the lion about the

time I went into labour.'

'The hell you did!'

'That you were mauled,' Cathy went on, as if she had not heard him. 'That you couldn't have been with me.' She stopped. When she went on again her voice was hardly louder than a whisper. 'Anyone could see that it wasn't your fault I lost the baby.'

For a long time Jarrod didn't speak. He seemed hardly to breathe. His body was taut with tension. A tension that communicated itself to Cathy. She hardly breathed herself as she waited for him to say something, anything.

'How long have you known?' he asked at last. His voice was harsh.

'A short while. Why didn't you tell me?'

'How long exactly?' he asked savagely.

A new Jarrod again. Every time she thought she understood him, she found that she did not understand him at all.

'Is it important?' she asked uncertainly.

'Very important.'

Her heart was beating fast, but she kept her voice calm. 'I think I began to suspect the truth when I saw the scars.'

'Not before?'

It really was important to him. Which answer did he want to hear? She had no way of knowing. She said truthfully, 'Not before then.'

He expelled a long breath. It was the answer he wanted, she thought, and wondered why.

'You couldn't have been sure though.' He was more subdued. 'It's one hell of a coincidence that the lion should have mauled me just at that time. How did you know, Cathy?'

After a moment she said, 'Amos told me.'

'Amos!'

'Only after I wormed it out of him.'

'When was that?'

'The same day I spoke to Stewart.'

'I see.'

'I wish I did.' Cathy pulled the sheet up to her chin. She was suddenly cold. 'It's your turn to do some talking.'

He did talk then. And from what he said Cathy was able to piece together a picture of what had happened. Some of it she already knew.

The lion had killed sheep on farms that neighboured the game-park. It had become necessary to go after it. There had been no thought then of killing the animal. The plan had been to trap it, and to transport it to wilder areas, or perhaps to a zoo.

'You didn't tell me,' Cathy said.

'I didn't want you to worry. You were so near the end of your pregnancy.'

But things had gone wrong. Amos and Jarrod had been ambushed by the animal, and they had been injured. For a long time they had been in hospital.

Cathy was stricken. 'You must have wondered why I never came to see you.'

'I nearly went out of my mind. I couldn't understand what had happened. Even at the lodges nobody knew where you were. There were no 'phone-calls, no letters. It was as if you'd disappeared off the face of the earth.'

'You didn't think of the flat?'

'I did. By then I was out of hospital and back at Marakizi. I spoke to the superintendent of the building. I drove all the way to the city and looked for myself. And I came up with nothing.'

'What did you think?' Cathy's voice was small.

'I didn't know what to think. I nearly went crazy with worry. I blamed you for walking out on me, and I blamed myself for not taking better care of you.'

'You weren't to blame.'

'In some ways I was.' Jarrod had grown reflective. 'You were too cut off here at Marakizi. You'd pleaded with me to have a 'phone installed, and I gave you back rubbish about not wanting the trappings of civilisation. Do you think I haven't kicked myself a thousand times for my stupidity?'

'You got the 'phone,' Cathy said slowly.

'And the helicopter. They were for you. I kept telling myself that some day you would come back to me. It was the only way I could keep my sanity.'

'And then I wrote you the letter.'

'The letter.' The rigidity was back in Jarrod's body. 'When I learned that you wanted a divorce my world was shattered.'

'You must have hated me.'

'I've never hated you, Cathy. I was exasperated and angry and frustrated. But I've never hated you.'

'And yet you wanted to see me suffer.'

'I've never wanted that.' A hand touched her face, the long fingers tugging gently at a damp tendril of hair. 'Don't you know why I didn't answer the letter? Why I insisted you stay a week before I'd give you that wretched consent?'

She turned her head to look at him. His eyes gleamed and his lips had lifted slightly at the corners. An unreasoning happiness began to burgeon inside her.

'Tell me,' she invited.

'Witch. When you look at me like that I don't feel in the least bit like talking, I just want to love you.' He gave the tendril of hair a tweak. 'By not answering I hoped you'd come here.'

'Which I did.'

'I hoped to make you stay forever.' He made a sound in his throat. 'You'll never know what I went through. Knowing you'd lost our baby. Seeing you with Stewart. Knowing you wanted to marry him. Wondering if I'd done the right thing, wondering if you'd remember that you'd loved me, or whether you'd end up hating me.' His voice turned husky. 'It was a gamble. But I was a desperate man.'

'And an unscrupulous one. You peppered me with all the ammunition at your disposal. Memories—oh, those memories. And your lovemaking. You knew Stewart could never make love to me like that. Didn't you have *any* scruples?' She ran a hand over his chest and felt his muscles tighten. 'After all, I was supposed to be engaged to another man.'

'No scruples,' he assured her.

'What would you have done if we'd both stayed the week?'

'It would have been a damned sight harder.'

'And at the end of it . . . What would have happened then?'

'I'd have refused the consent.'

She stared at him. 'But you promised.'

The grin he gave her was wicked. 'Don't you know, my darling, that there's no fairness in love or war? This was both.'

'Stewart never stood a chance against you. My poor Stewart.'

'Poor man, I agree. But the other way it would have been poor Cathy and poor Jarrod. And that would have been infinitely worse.'

'Oh yes, it would have been.' Cathy was thoughtful. 'I feel very bad about Stewart, I wasn't fair to him, I should have known all the time . . . There's a girl, Jarrod, she loves him, her name is Anna, and he went out with her a few times before he met me. I hope . . .' She stopped, 'I never slept with Stewart. Ever.'

'You said . . .'

'It wasn't true. But you and Helen . . .'

'Helen sketched for me. Nothing else. There's never been anyone but you, Cathy, since the day you came to me after the lecture.' He kissed her lingeringly. 'I fell in love with you then, and I've never stopped loving you.'

For a long time they lay together, in a closeness

that was like old times, and yet so much more precious—for they knew how close they'd come to losing it.

At length Cathy asked, 'Why didn't you tell me about the mauling? You listened to my accusations, and you didn't say a word about the lion. Jarrod, why?'

'Would it have made a difference if I had?'

Beside her the long body had stiffened. Cathy said, 'Of course!'

'Which is why I didn't say anything.' Jarrod kissed a tantalising trail around her lips. Then he said, 'Don't you understand, my dearest?'

Dimly, very dimly, she was beginning to understand. 'You didn't want me to know.'

'I didn't want you to feel sorry for me. One word about the accident and you might have left Stewart and come back to me.'

That was exactly what she would have done. 'Yes ...'

'That wasn't what I wanted,' Jarrod said fiercely. 'Your sympathy. It had to be your love, or nothing at all.'

'That's why it was so important for you to know *when* I found out about the lion.'

'Precisely.'

'My darling,' she said urgently, 'the morning we made love—I knew then how I felt about you. I hadn't spoken to Amos yet, but I knew that I had never stopped loving you. I knew I'd never go to Stewart.'

'Cathy, my darling Cathy.' His voice was sombre. 'Can there be more babies?'

'The doctor said yes.'

'Why don't we start one now?'

'Your arm ...'

He laughed softly. 'Did you let that get in your way the last time? Cathy—let's.'

And they did.

Coming Next Month in Harlequin Presents!

863 MATCHING PAIR Jayne Bauling
A lounge singer and a hotel owner are two of a kind. He chooses to live life on the surface; she feels she has no choice. Neither have been touched by love.

864 SONG OF A WREN Emma Darcy
Her friend and lodger, a terrible tease, introduces her to his family in Sydney as his "live-in lady." No wonder his brother deliberately downplays their immediate attraction.

865 A MAN WORTH KNOWING Alison Fraser
A man worth knowing, indeed! An English secretary decides that an American author is not worth getting involved with...as if the choice is hers to make.

866 DAUGHTER OF THE SEA Emma Goldrick
A woman found washed ashore on a French Polynesian island feigns amnesia. Imagine her shock when her rescuer insists that she's his wife, the mother of his little girl!

867 ROSES, ALWAYS ROSES Claudia Jameson
Roses aren't welcome from the businessman a London *pâtisserie* owner blames for her father's ruin. She rejects his company, but most of all she rejects his assumption that her future belongs with him.

868 PERMISSION TO LOVE Penny Jordan
Just when a young woman resigns herself to a passionless marriage to satisfy her father's will, the man in charge of her fortune and her fate withholds his approval.

869 PALE ORCHID Anne Mather
When a relative of his wrongs her sister, a secretary confronts the Hawaiian millionaire who once played her for a fool. She expects him to be obstructive—not determined to win her back.

870 A STRANGER'S TOUCH Sophie Weston
One-night stands are not her style. Yet a young woman cannot deny being deeply touched by the journalist who stops by her English village to recover from one of his overseas assignments.

Can you keep a secret?

You can keep this one plus 4 free novels